ANIMATING MARIA

If you have a wild, unruly, or undisciplined daughter, two ladies of genteel birth offer to bring out said daughter and refine what may have seemed unrefinable. We can make the best of the worst.

Amy and Effy Tribble place this advertisement in the *Morning Post* and hire themselves out as chaperones to prepare difficult young misses for marriage, educating them in their School of Manners. Maria Kendall is beautiful, delightfully mannered, graceful and the Tribble sisters think they will have no problem securing her a duke. They have not, however, reckoned on her boorish, vulgar parents...

ANIMATING MARIA

ANIMATING MARIA

by

M. C. Beaton

Magna Large Print Books
Long Preston, North Yorkshire,
BD23 4ND, England.

British Library Cataloguing in Publication Data.

Beaton, M. C.
    Animating Maria.

    A catalogue record of this book is
    available from the British Library

    ISBN   978-0-7505-3760-5

First published in 1990 in the US by St Martin's Press,
this edition is published by Canvas by
Constable & Robinson Ltd., 2012

Published in Large Print 2013 by arrangement with
Constable & Robinson Ltd.

Magna Large Print is an imprint of Library Magna Books Ltd.

Printed and bound in Great Britain by
T.J. (International) Ltd., Cornwall, PL28 8RW

1

*Father, O Father! what do we here
In this land of unbelief and fear?
The Land of Dreams is better far
Above the light of the morning star.*

William Blake

'Common as a barber's chair,' said Miss Amy Tribble.

'But so exquisitely pretty,' pointed out her sister, Effy. 'Quite the prettiest to have engaged our services.'

The Tribble sisters were discussing their latest 'client', Maria Kendall. Although they were good *ton*, the sisters were always in need of money, and sponsoring 'difficult' girls at the Season had proved a lucrative source of income. The Tribbles were too eccentric to attract the attentions of any match-making mama with a sweet young thing to puff off. But parents of the spoilt, the rowdy, the farouche, or the downright odd turned to the Tribbles. Despite four previous successes, they were lucky to get any clients, because it seemed their tall house in Holles Street in the West End of London attracted murder and mayhem.

They also had a resident French dress-maker, but it had become well known that Yvette had given birth to an illegitimate child, a child the Tribbles had not only let her have in their house but had also announced their intention of looking after.

So the fact that the Kendalls stank of the shop and were incredibly vulgar did not stop the Tribble sisters from thinking they were very lucky to get anyone at all.

Thanks to their previous successes, their home was now well appointed and well run. The drawing room in which the sisters sat, discussing the Kendalls and the imminent arrival of their daughter Maria, was a pretty room with long windows boasting new gold-and-white-striped curtains. The furniture had been upholstered in gold-and-white satin, and a fine Aubusson carpet covered the floor. The furniture was a pleasant mixture of the old and the new. There were books and magazines, vases of flowers and the scent of applewood from a cheerful fire.

Both spinsters were reputed to be in their fifties. Effy Tribble, who had been plain in her youth, had become a pretty, dainty woman with silver-white hair, a sweet face and a trim figure. Her twin, Amy, was less favoured. She had a sad, horselike face, a flat figure, large feet, and was often clumsy.

They were jealous of each other. Amy envied Effy's looks, and Effy envied the way Amy seemed to get the gentlemen to like her. Until the last Season, they had competed for the attentions of their nabob friend, Mr Haddon. But now Mr Haddon's friend, Mr Randolph, was on the scene. He had also returned from India rich and still a bachelor.

The sisters had spent many, many Seasons in London, but age had not diminished their hopes of marriage. Despite wrinkles and back pains and sagging skin on the outside, a young and tremulous girl still lived inside each of them, longing for a husband.

But that afternoon, they had for once put all thoughts of their own romantic dreams out of their heads. Maria Kendall meant work, and work meant money. The vulgar Kendalls had already paid out a large sum of money in advance.

'The parents may be pushy, mushroom sort of people,' said Effy, 'but you must admit that Maria Kendall is as graceful and charming as she is beautiful.'

11

'When she's actually *there*,' said Amy crossly. 'Her parents say she lives in a dream-world and no amount of whipping will bring her down to earth.'

'On the other hand, does she need to be brought down to earth?' asked Effy. 'She is rich and beautiful.'

'But think of our reputation,' pointed out Amy. 'We have secured titled gentlemen for all our previous charges. Any lord has only to meet Maria's father and mother to take the whole family in dislike. Do you know that Mr Kendall told me the price of every item in that dreadful drawing room of theirs?'

'Yes,' said Effy. 'And Mrs Kendall had her jewel box brought in and discussed the value of every stone with me. Where does their money come from again?'

'Coal mines,' said Amy gloomily.

'So low,' mourned Effy. 'Now tea or beer would have been quite respectable, but there is nothing respectable about coal.'

'The Tribbles have never been in trade,' said Amy.

'We are now, dear,' said Effy sweetly. 'And if Papa had been a low sort of gentleman in trade, we might have been set up for life.'

'Nonsense. Papa could have gambled coal

mines away with the same ease as he gambled his estates away. There is one good thing about Maria; she does seem to be very accomplished. Her needlework is exquisite, her water-colours are good enough, and her piano playing is a delight.'

'Can she dance well, d'you think?'

'Bound to,' said Amy. 'She moves so gracefully.'

'At least Mr and Mrs Kendall are not accompanying her to London. They've hired some shabby genteel Bath spinster to accompany her. What is her name? Ah, Miss Spiggs. I hope this Miss Spiggs realizes she cannot stay in London and her services are at an end as soon as she delivers Maria.'

'If she doesn't know, we'll soon tell her,' said Amy grimly. 'At least Maria is travelling from Bath. A good hard road and little fear of footpads and highwaymen. We may complain about the Kendalls, but we need their money. I only hope that dreamaday Jill doesn't wander off somewhere on the road and forget she's supposed to be travelling to London!'

Miss Maria Kendall had little hope of forgetting where she was bound. She was travelling in a brand-new travelling carriage with Miss Spiggs, her lady's maid, Betty, two outriders, two grooms on the backstrap, and a coachman and burly thug hired for her protection on the box.

For the moment, as the grey, depressing countryside rolled past outside the carriage, Maria was not lost in dreams or fancies. Her thoughts were of a more practical nature. She hated every bit of the wardrobe her mother had chosen for her. Her gowns were too jeune fille, too high-necked and frilled and tucked and gored. She was a good needlewoman and when they stopped for the night, she planned to sit up and alter at least one gown to make it look more like one of the illustrations in *La Belle Assemblée* and less like those made-up gowns which provincial dressmakers put in their shop windows to advertise their skills. Mrs Kendall had no eye for line, no eye for fashion. As long as the material cost the earth, she felt happy about the result.

The steady drizzle which had been falling all day changed to heavy rain. Rain thudded down on the carriage roof and lashed against the windows.

'I wonder if John Coachman can get us to The Bell by nightfall,' Miss Spiggs asked anxiously. The Bell was where they were to

14

break their journey for the night. It was a famous and luxurious posting-house. Miss Spiggs had never been used to any luxury at all and had been looking forward to that posting-house all day.

'Ask him then,' said Maria.

Miss Spiggs got to her feet and balanced in the swaying coach, pushing open the trap in the roof with her cane. A small waterfall poured down on her and she gasped and spluttered. Maria turned away to hide a smile. She thought Miss Spiggs a detestable creature. Miss Spiggs was a small plump lady in her late twenties with mousy-brown hair, a round face, pale-blue eyes, and a little curved mouth like those mouths you see on eighteenth-century statues. She had a sycophantic, oily manner and was not very clean. Her gown stank of benzine from frequent cleanings, her armpits of sweat and her feet of old unwashed stockings. It was, Maria reflected gleefully, probably the first wash Miss Spiggs had had in months. While Miss Spiggs sank back in the seat, leaving the trap open, Maria stood up and called out to the coachman, who replied they were nearly at their destination. Maria closed the trap and sat down.

'Dearie me, Miss Kendall,' said Miss

Spiggs. 'I am quite wet.'

'What you need,' said Maria firmly, 'is a warm bath as soon as we arrive.'

'I do not hold with bathing all over,' said Miss Spiggs. 'It can cause the ague.'

'Nonsense,' said Maria robustly.

'I do not know what Mrs Kendall will say when she hears about this,' sniffed Miss Spiggs. 'She don't hold with washing all over.'

'But I do,' said Maria sweetly, 'and you are now under my orders. Do I make myself clear?'

'Of course, of course, my dear Miss Kendall. Anything you want. You have only to command. I am only a poor creature of aristocratic birth who has fallen on hard times and I often forget my lowly station. Oh, my poor papa. He must be revolving in his grave.'

Maria reflected that she had now heard of Mr Spigg's revolving so many times that the corpse must surely have dug a hole right down to Australia by now. She pictured an angry and earth-covered Mr Spiggs erupting in the middle of a convict settlement. Maria's thoughts drifted on. It would be fun to sail across the world to Australia. The sun shone there, it was said. The captain of the

16

ship would be a tall man with thick black hair, merry blue eyes and a tanned face. He would fall in love with her. They would be married on board ship. The pirates would attack them and he would defend his ship nobly, saving them all at the last minute, except Miss Spiggs, whom the pirates had made to walk the plank just before the gallant captain's rescue. Maria and the captain would build a fine house in Australia and have parrots and monkeys. Did they have monkeys in Australia? Well, if they didn't, the captain would ship them in for her amusement. But there were all those convicts about. That could not be so terrible, decided Maria after much hard thought. People were transported for all sorts of minor crimes, like stealing loaves of bread. Convicts might be quite jolly. Any company seemed jolly after Bath society. And anyone who had survived transportation was bound to be healthy, not like all those invalids who invaded the Pump Room in Bath, comparing physical deformities and sores. Back to the gallant captain. She had married him but he had not even kissed her yet. What would that be like? It was very hard to imagine being kissed when no one had kissed you.

The carriage lurched to a halt. They had

arrived. Maria was disappointed to have to give up such a splendid dream.

There seemed to be a great number of people and carriages about the inn. As the groom let down the steps, he said, 'They're saying as how part of the road is washed away up ahead. We may not be able to travel on tomorrow.'

'Very well,' said Maria, climbing down. 'It does not matter all that much. This posting-house has a good reputation and will be a comfortable place to stay.'

But Maria, who was all ready to sink back into her pleasant dream about the captain, received a rude shock when she walked into the hall of the posting-house. She found she had to share a room not only with her maid but with Miss Spiggs as well.

'And why is that, sir?' demanded Maria. 'My parents bespoke two bedchambers, one for me and one for my companion and lady's maid.'

The owner, Mr Swan, bowed low. 'I am sorry, miss, but there are so many travellers stranded by the weather. The Duke of Berham himself arrived looking for a room and I could hardly refuse.'

'Oh yes, you could,' said Maria crossly. 'Very well, see to it that an extra room is found as soon as you possibly can, for it seems as if we shall be stranded here for more than one night.'

But Maria became even more angry when she saw the room. There was a large four-poster bed and a truckle-bed in the corner. She summoned Mr Swan and demanded another bed to be set up in the room. Maria had no intention of sharing a bed with Miss Spiggs.

'And,' she called to the owner's retreating back, 'have a bath of hot water sent up immediately.'

He swung round. 'I will send it up as soon as it is free.'

'I want it *now*,' said Maria, thinking that Miss Spiggs now smelled like a wet dog.

'I am afraid it has just been taken up to the Duke of Berham's room,' said Mr Swan miserably.

'And everything must be for the Duke of Berham? Very well, as soon as you can. We are all hungry. Where is my private parlour?'

Mr Swan turned red. 'His grace demanded a private parlour and–'

'If there was anywhere else to stay on this dreadful night, then I would find it, you toady,' said Maria. 'Go and tell this duke I want that parlour.'

The owner looked at this Miss Kendall's provincial clothes. He cringed before her rage but a duke was a duke. 'I am afraid I cannot do that,' he said. 'I shall put screens around a table in the public dining-room.'

Maria felt the lack of male support keenly. This owner would not have been so ready to give up the private parlour if she had been a man. 'I told his grace you had already bespoken it,' said Mr Swan in a conciliatory tone, 'but he reminded me he owns most of the land around here, including the land on which this posting-house stands. I am sorry we had to give the Blue Room to him instead of you.'

'Thank you, that will be all,' said Maria, suddenly realizing the futility of arguing with him any further.

But when the bath finally arrived and a protesting and screaming Miss Spiggs was shoved into it by a determined Maria, she found her rage against this high-handed duke mounting by the minute. She went through Miss Spiggs's trunk while Betty, the maid, scrubbed that lady's back, or as much of it as she could considering Miss Spiggs had insisted on taking a bath in her shift. Then, piling up an armful of clothes, she rang the bell and handed them to a chambermaid, with instructions that everything was to be laundered.

'What am I to wear?' moaned Miss Spiggs.

'I have left a gown out for you,' said Maria, 'and a clean shift which you will need to sleep in tonight, for I have sent your night-gowns to the laundry as well. When were your clothes last laundered?'

'On laundry day,' said Miss Spiggs. 'The beginning of February.'

'And this is the beginning of April,' pointed out Maria. She changed out of her travelling-gown into one of her plainer gowns of striped merino wool.

'Wait here for me,' she said.

'Where are you going, miss?' asked Betty.

'To see the Duke of Berham and give him a piece of my mind!'

Maria stopped a chambermaid outside and asked for the Blue Room and was told it was next door. She knocked on the door and, when there was no reply, tried the handle. The door was not locked. She opened it and walked in.

The Duke of Berham was attired only in his small-clothes. He was naked to the waist and sitting at the toilet table brushing his hair. He had sent his valet along to the parlour to supervise the laying of dinner.

Maria stood in the doorway and glared at him. The fact that he really looked like a duke and not like a coal-heaver, which was what most dukes seemed to look like, did not calm her anger or intimidate her. He had very thick fair hair, almost white, and large black eyes under heavy lids, a proud nose, a firm mouth, and a square chin. His muscled chest was white and hairless and his shoulders broad.

The duke for his part saw in his mirror a very pretty girl standing glaring at him. She had thick chestnut hair with gold threads that shone in the candlelight. Her eyes were green, her face sweet, and her pink mouth as perfectly shaped as her figure in the merino gown.

He turned and stood up, and looked down his nose at her, his hands on his hips.

'Well?' he demanded.

'Insufferable pompous lout,' said Maria, her temper snapping. 'I ordered this room for my maid and companion and I ordered a private parlour which you have calmly taken away from me.'

'You are impertinent. Who are you?'

'I am Miss Maria Kendall of Bath and I demand that private parlour back again.'

'Don't your parents know any better than

to let you go wandering into strange inn rooms?' he demanded. 'I am in my buffs, or had you not noticed?'

'Only half of you is naked,' said Maria. 'My parents are not with me.'

'That is a pity, otherwise I could have called on them and told them exactly what I think of your behaviour,' said the duke. 'Be off with you.'

'Not until you have at least apologized.'

'I have no intention of apologizing to a minx like you. Take yourself off.'

'No,' said Maria stubbornly.

'It is as well I am a gentleman, Miss Kendall, or you might learn a sharp lesson in what happens to misses who accost half-naked gentlemen in their bedchambers.'

'You are no gentleman, sir. You are a pompous idiot and you look quite stupid prancing about in only your drawers, trying to lay down the law.'

No one had ever dared to speak to the great Duke of Berham in such a manner.

He strode up to her, jerked her into his arms and forced his mouth down on her own. She wriggled against him, trying to get free, but the more she wriggled against his bare chest, the deeper and more searching that kiss became. Maria decided to stay passive in his arms until he had finished. His kiss became gentler, more caressing. She saw her opportunity, wrenched herself out of his arms and stood there, face flaming, green eyes as bright and hard as emeralds.

'You shall answer for this insult,' she said, taking out a handkerchief and scrubbing her mouth.

'Are you going to call me out, Miss Kendall?'

'My fiancé will.'

'And who is this fiancé?'

Maria thought of the captain of her recent dream. 'Captain Jack Freemantle of the good ship *Mary Bess*,' she said.

'And when may I expect to be challenged to a duel?'

'As soon as he returns from Australia.'

'Then I await his return.'

Maria went out and slammed the door behind her. She leaned against the wall, her heart thudding. What had she done? As soon as she saw him in his undress, she should have blushed in a maidenly manner and then waited outside until he had dressed.

She swung about. 'Damn you, sir,' said Maria Kendall furiously and kicked the closed door of his room.

She then made her way to her own room.

24

Miss Spiggs was dressed and shivering beside the fire. Two chambermaids and two waiters were carrying out the bath. Maria averted her eyes from the dirty water.

'I feel I must write to Mrs Kendall of your behaviour, Miss Kendall,' said Miss Spiggs in a stifled voice. 'Just because I am fallen on hard times, there is no need for you to treat me in such a manner.'

'If I have to share the same room as you,' said Maria, 'then there is every reason to treat you in such a manner.'

'I have never been so humiliated in my life,' wailed Miss Spiggs.

Maria's face softened. 'Do not take on so, Miss Spiggs. You have been living alone for some time now, have you not? It is not your fault. You could not possibly know how smelly you had become.' She went over to her jewel box, ferreted about and finally drew out a handsome diamond pin. 'You may have this, Miss Spiggs. It will look very fine on your gown.'

'Oh, thank you,' breathed Miss Spiggs, staring in awe at the sparkling diamond. 'You must forgive me for being so upset, Miss Kendall. Of course you have the right of it. My poor neglected solitary life. If only Mr Spiggs could see me now in the lowly position of companion, he would—'

'Yes, he would turn in his grave,' sighed Maria. There came a scratching at the door. Maria opened it. A liveried footman stood there. He bowed low. 'The Duke of Berham's compliments,' he said. 'His grace would be honoured if Miss Kendall would join him for dinner.'

'Tell the Duke of Berham I have no wish to join him,' said Maria, her face flaming as she remembered that kiss.

The footman bowed and walked away.

Maria's temper was soothed by the excellence of the fare served in the dining room. The first course consisted of carrot soup à la Creole, soup à la Reine, baked cod, and stewed eels. The entrée boasted riz de veau and tomato sauce, vol-au-vent of chicken, pork cutlets and sauce Robert, and grilled mushrooms. The second course was rump of beef à la jardiniere, roast goose, boiled fowls and celery sauce, garnished tongue and vegetables. The third course offered grouse and pheasants, quince jelly, lemon cream, apple tart, compote of peaches, Nesselrode pudding, cabinet pudding, and scalloped oysters. Then followed fruit and ices.

'A delicate repast and elegant sufficiency,'

said Miss Spiggs, dabbing her mouth with her napkin. Her eyes were bulging, as if all the food inside her were putting pressure on them. She was so well pleased with her present of the diamond pin that she even forgave Maria for ordering the maid, Betty, to sit down at table with them, Maria pointing out that, as they were screened from the rest of the dining room, they did not need to follow convention. Their table was set in the bay of a window, and outside the rain drummed down with remorseless fury.

There came a great deal of noise and argument from the dining room as more travellers arrived demanding to be served. Maria heard one man say that part of the road had been washed away and no one knew when they would be able to resume their journey.

Maria frowned. She did not want to be trapped in this inn with the Duke of Berham. She wanted to forget him. He had behaved disgracefully, and she had no man to support her and exact revenge for that kiss. She fell to dreaming about the captain again, wishing he were not a figment of her imagination. But, unlike other times, the dream did not comfort her. The duke's handsome and haughty face kept interrupting it. She began to dream of revenge instead.

She had never consciously tried to attract any man; such suitors as she did have she had always considered an unwelcome interruption to whatever dream she had wrapped round her. The fact was that Maria had been overbullied by her parents since an early age and had learned to escape from them in rosy fantasies. What if she could make this duke fall in love with her and then spurn him? It would do no harm to find out a little more about him.

When the meal was over, she sent Miss Spiggs and Betty upstairs and sought out the landlord, Mr Swan, and complimented him on his chef. Mr Swan beamed. He had been sure Maria was going to complain about the duke.

'We keep a good kitchen, miss,' he said. 'Travellers come from all over to stay here.'

'And from quite near too,' said Maria. 'The Duke of Berham owns the land on which this inn stands and so he must live hard by.'

'A few miles from here, miss. But, like yourself, he was caught in the storm. Bound for London is his grace.'

'He seems a cold and proud and arrogant man, from what I have heard,' pursued Maria.

'Very lofty in his ways,' agreed the landlord, 'but he *is* a duke.'

'I though that after the experience of the American colonial wars and the French bourgeois rebellion the English aristocrat would have been more careful not to appear autocratic,' said Maria.

'Well, they was for a bit,' agreed Mr Swan. 'But now it looks as if no one's going to hang them from the lamp-post, so they're free to go back to their old ways.'

'No doubt his duchess is equally haughty.'

'His grace is not married. 'Tis said he claims he cannot find a lady to suit him. Lor', there's many that have tried. I'm sorry about your extra bedchamber and that private parlour, but there was no stopping him.' Mr Swan laughed. 'You should have heard him. "Who is this Miss Kendall?" he says, looking down his nose at me. "I am surprised, Swan, that you should put the comforts of a nobody above those of myself."'

The landlord laughed, and Maria gritted her teeth. 'Still, stands to reason,' the inn-keeper went on, 'him owning all the land. He even goes on as if he's running this inn. Says if the weather continues bad tomorrow, he's going to organize a dance in the assembly rooms at the back.'

'Well, let's hope the weather clears,' said

Maria, 'for I am anxious to be on my way. The people who are waiting for me in London will wonder what has happened to me.'

'It's bound to be in the newspapers,' said the landlord soothingly, 'that's if the towers hasn't been washed away.' He meant the observation towers strung across the country, where news was signalled from one to the other and so to the capital.

'I hope so,' said Maria. 'Good evening, Mr Swan.'

She went up to her room and sat patiently while Betty brushed her hair. Miss Spiggs chattered on about this and that, but her voice buzzed only faintly in Maria's ears. If this ball did take place and if she wished to attract the duke with a view to getting her revenge, she could hardly do so with the wardrobe she possessed.

'Get me out the white muslin ball-gown,' she said to Betty, 'and bring me my work-basket.'

Maria looked gloomily at the gown. It had puffed sleeves and a high neckline and screamed provincial from every seam. She took out a small pair of scissors and began to pick the seams apart. 'Get me that green silk frock, Betty,' she ordered. 'This dress needs a bit of trimming.'

'I do not think your mama would like you to touch that gown,' said Miss Spiggs severely. 'She considered that gown very suitable for a young lady making her début.'

Maria paid her no heed. She began to cut and stitch, glancing all the while at the open pages of an issue of *La Belle Assemblée* she had brought with her.

Miss Spiggs finally undressed and went to bed, still grumbling as she fell asleep. Maria drew a branch of candles closer to her and continued to work.

Amy, Effy, Mr Haddon and Mr Randolph were playing a rubber of whist. Amy was abstracted and had to keep being called to order. At last she threw down her cards. 'It's that wretched girl,' she mourned. 'The papers say the roads are washed away. Goodness knows what she is getting up to. People like the Kendalls will consider it our responsibility if anything happens to her, even though she never reached here. And who are we to find for her? Only think of those parents. Do you think we might get her married off by persuading them not to attend the ceremony?'

'Do not be ridiculous,' said Effy. 'Mr and Mrs Kendall's sole ambition is to have their daughter married well and to be present at the wedding.'

'All you ladies do is think of weddings,' teased Mr Randolph.

Amy rounded on him, her eyes flashing. 'And why not, sir? What in the name of the devil's backside are such as Maria Kendall to do? If she does not marry, her life will go on a vulgar hell of bullying to the grave.'

'Let us hope she knows how to charm the gentlemen,' murmured Effy slyly. 'Your farouche behaviour has not been exactly successful, sis.'

Such a snide remark in front of two gentlemen, two *eligible* gentlemen, left Amy breathless.

Mr Haddon said severely, 'We are not discussing Miss Amy, Miss Effy, although many gentlemen such as myself find Miss Amy's honest and direct manners a welcome relief from simpering and giggling. We are discussing the marital hopes of a young girl of unfortunate parents. My advice is not to look too high. There are many fine men in the merchant class.'

Effy bridled. 'We do not know such persons.'

'You know me.'

'My dear Mr Haddon, no one considers

the East India Company to be *trade*.'

'You are in trade yourself,' went on Mr Haddon, showing an unexpected glimmer of malice. 'You advertise for young girls.'

'That is a genteel occupation,' said Effy, becoming tearful. 'What has come over you, Mr Haddon? You are *attacking* me.'

'Steady, Haddon,' murmured Mr Randolph. 'You are being too hard on Miss Effy. Do not cry, Miss Effy, or you will make your eyes red.'

This had the effect of drying Effy's tears. The game continued with some semblance of friendliness. But Amy was worried. Never before had Effy been quite so openly malicious. Did Mr Haddon and Mr Randolph not realize they were still marriageable and that the two poor spinster Tribbles looked on them as their last hope? Amy then thought of Mr Haddon's compliment but it did not warm her. He had leaped to her defence as a good friend should, but Amy longed for something warmer than friendliness. She thought of all those London Seasons stretching back down the years, Seasons where she and Effy had sat on the edge of the ballroom floor, hoping and hoping. Every winter hope had died only to spring again, phoenix-like, from the ashes as a new Season began.

Amy suddenly had a very clear picture of how the pair of them must have looked to society in the more recent years, two spinsters still acting like young hopefuls, two objects of pity. She suddenly covered her face with her hand of cards and began to cry.

'I am a wicked woman,' screamed Effy. 'I have hurt you. Oh, forgive me, sis.' And Effy began to cry as well. Mr Haddon patted Amy on the back, recommended brandy, gave her a clean handkerchief, and then sat down and began to cry himself, as any gentleman of sensibility ought to do. Not to be outdone, Mr Randolph sobbed with little snuffling noises into a fine cambric handkerchief, and the tears rained down from the eyes of all until the cards on the table became quite damp.

'A pox on this,' said Amy at last. 'Let's have some champagne and forget the Kendall girl. She's probably dreaming so hard, she don't know what day of the week it is!'

2

Vengeance, deep-brooding o'er the slain,
Had lock'd the source of softer woe;
And burning pride and high disdain
Forbade the rising tear to flow.

Sir Walter Scott

The next day, the rain ceased, although a sullen grey sky still pressed down on the sodden fields about the inn. Maria went for a walk along the road with Miss Spiggs to view the ravages of the storm. They had gone only a little way when Miss Spiggs began to complain that her feet hurt. Maria longed to send her back and walk ahead on her own, but she knew she ought to be chaperoned, and although she still fiercely blamed the Duke of Berham, the thought of her own behaviour made her blush. She should never have gone to see him on her own. When she saw him half-naked, she should have fled. So she ignored Miss Spiggs's complaints and picked her way along the muddy road, holding up her skirts.

They had gone about half a mile when they came to a raging torrent which cut across the road and plunged down a rocky slope into the tangled briers and scrub of an uncultivated field below.

A knot of people were already there, staring at the flood in dismay. One of them, a gentlewoman who was there with her maid, turned round as Maria approached and exclaimed, 'They say we will be stranded at the inn until this torrent abates. Perhaps it is as well we have the Duke of Berham to provide for our amusement.'

'And how is his grace going to do that?' asked Maria, wondering if there was to be some diversion other than the proposed dance.

'He is giving a ball in the assembly room tonight and as the road north between the inn and his estates is clear, he has sent for his staff to help with the arrangements.'

Maria stiffened. 'If the road to his home is clear, why does not the duke return there and leave room at the inn for travellers?'

'I think he feels it his duty to plan amusement for us, as we are on his land,' said the lady. 'We must introduce ourselves. I am Miss Frederica Sunningdale.'

Maria, introducing herself in turn, saw that the face peering out at her from the shadow of a great poke-bonnet was young and pretty. 'Do your parents accompany you, Miss Sunningdale?' she asked.

'Oh, yes. Papa and Mama are in high alt. They are taking me to London for the Season, but they have high hopes that I will entrap the duke. There are not many young ladies at the inn. I had hoped for a clear field, but you are very pretty,' said Miss Sunningdale candidly, 'and so I shall have to battle for his attention.'

Maria was about to say huffily that she had no interest in engaging the Duke of Berham's affections but remembered just in time her plan to ensnare him and then repulse him. Instead she said, 'His grace seems too lofty and proud to consider any young lady good enough for him.'

'The way I see it,' said Miss Sunningdale earnestly, 'is that he is quite old. In his thirties. That is the time when bachelors suddenly decide to marry. One has only to be there at the right time, if you see what I mean.'

Maria grinned. 'Then let us hope this is the right time for you too, Miss Sunningdale.'

They turned about to walk back to the inn.

Miss Spiggs hesitated. She longed to have a comfortable gossip with Miss Sunningdale's maid and yet felt she would be lowering herself by doing so. But both Maria and Miss Sunningdale were walking at a brisk pace and so she contented herself by limping behind and pretending the Sunningdale maid did not exist.

'Are you bound for London as well?' asked Miss Sunningdale.

'Yes,' said Maria.

'With your parents?'

'No, I am being sent to the Tribble sisters in Holles Street.'

'I have heard of them,' remarked Miss Sunningdale cautiously. 'But you look like a terribly nice lady to me.'

'Which means?'

'The Tribble sisters advertise their services. They say they can manage difficult misses.'

'Oh,' said Maria in a worried voice. 'Is that generally known?'

'Yes, for they are highly successful. But there has been murder done in that house, and all sorts of exciting mayhem. I do envy you. Are you very wicked?' she asked hopefully.

'Not in the slightest,' retorted Maria. 'My parents do not feel up to the task of puffing me off and so engaged the Tribbles. That is all.'

'Pity. I have never met anyone wicked.'

'And do you want to?'

'Oh, yes. Life is so very dull. Nothing exciting ever happens.'

'This is an adventure,' pointed out Maria. 'You are stranded in an inn with a handsome duke.'

'Of course you are right. Perhaps I am just stupid. Perhaps all sorts of wildly exciting things happen to me, only I do not notice them.'

They walked amicably together to the inn and Maria proposed they should have some refreshment in the coffee room. She dismissed Miss Spiggs with relief.

As they sat down together, Maria wondered what Miss Sunningdale really looked like. The poke of her bonnet was so deep, it was like peering down a tunnel.

'I feel we shall become friends,' said Maria's new companion. 'You may call me Frederica.'

'And I am Maria. Tell me, Frederica, what do you plan to wear to this ball?'

'I have a very beautiful gown. Pale-blue muslin. Do you think the duke will like pale blue?'

'I am sure he will,' said Maria.

'The trouble is,' said Frederica, taking little birdlike sips of coffee and then putting the cup down and staring at Maria earnestly, 'I am not up to the weight of the duke. My father is a rector and although we are going to stay with my godmother, Lady Bentley, who is very grand, I do not have a very large dowry.'

'The duke is surely very rich.'

'Indeed, yes, Maria. But when did even a rich aristocrat marry anyone without much money?'

'I do not know. My parents are not of the first stare, or,' added Maria gloomily, 'of the second.'

'Never mind,' said Frederica. 'There are so many gentlemen here and so few ladies that we shall be the belles of the ball. Good gracious! Here is the duke himself.'

Maria looked up quickly. The duke, accompanied by two gentlemen, had just walked into the coffee room. He was taller and grander than Maria remembered. He was wearing a curly brimmed beaver on his head and had a many-caped coat slung about his shoulders. He talked for a few moments to his companions and glanced about the coffee room. His eye fell on the two girls and he recognized Maria.

But his gaze was cold and indifferent. He did not even nod. He turned about and left the room with the two men following him.

'Oh, dear,' said Frederica bleakly. 'Not much hope there.'

Maria nodded and drank her coffee while inwardly fuming. Then a smile curled her lips. He could hardly avoid her that evening. There just weren't enough ladies to go around.

After dinner, Maria was helped into her ball-gown by Betty. Betty was in raptures over the transformation but Miss Spiggs held up her hands in shock. The neckline was too low, she said. And all that green silk embellishment! So common!

'Stow it,' said Maria with a bluntness worthy of Miss Amy Tribble. She twisted this way and that in front of the glass. The new neckline of the gown was edged with green silk leaves which she had cut out of the green silk gown. The same leaves formed a band about the sleeves and decorated the hem between the flounces. Betty arranged the green silk roses Maria had made in her hair and then clasped a necklace of coral about her neck.

There came a great commotion from the

courtyard outside. Maria went to the window, opened it and leaned out. Carriage after carriage was arriving in the courtyard below and ladies were descending, beautiful and groomed ladies, expensively gowned ladies, dipping their feathered heads as they climbed down from the carriages, lifting their skirts high above the mud of the yard with a prancing step, like circus ponies, thought Maria.

Maria drew her head in and rang the bell. After some time, a breathless chambermaid answered its summons and to Maria's questions replied that the Dowager Duchess of Berham had been entertaining a large party of friends and they had all decided to drive over and attend the ball. A great matchmaker was the old duchess, said the chambermaid. She never gave up trying to find a bride for her son and kept inviting some of the fairest ladies in the land in the hope of persuading her son to marry one of them.

Maria thanked her and then sat down. She smoothed down her gown with a nervous hand. Was it too provincial? Would these grand ladies recognize a provincial gown hurriedly made over?

The sheer idea of the duke even asking her for one dance now seemed ridiculous.

'I think it is time we left,' said Miss Spiggs. She was wearing a mud-coloured gown and a pleated cap of depressing grey georgette. Maria thought her companion looked as inspiring as a rainy day.

'Where is the diamond pin I gave you?' asked Maria.

'I put it away safely,' said Miss Spiggs. 'Someone might snatch it from my bosom at the ball.'

Maria giggled at the thought of anyone being bold enough even to approach Miss Spiggs's formidable bosom. Miss Spiggs's breasts were pushed up so high by her whalebone corsets that she looked as if her chin were resting on a mud-coloured pillow.

They made their way downstairs to the assembly room at the back of the inn. Banks of hothouse flowers from the duke's estate scented the air. Masses of candles were blazing and a large fire had been lit at either end of the room.

Not only the duke and his mother's friends were present along with the stranded travellers at the inn, but everyone else from the villages round about. It was to be a real country ball, run on democratic lines that would have shocked London society had it taken place at, say, Almack's. A country dance was in progress. The major-domo was calling out cheerfully, 'Cross hands and down the middle,' and a flushed and sweating farmer was leading an elegant and aristocratic lady down the set.

Maria looked about for Frederica Sunningdale but did not see her.

Then she felt a hand on her arm. 'Maria,' said a voice. 'It is not so very frightening after all. There are quite a lot of very common people here.'

Maria turned about. Without her poke-bonnet, Frederica was revealed as a very pretty girl. She had a glossy mop of jet-black curls, wide blue eyes, and a neat figure.

'Let us find somewhere to sit down,' said Maria, 'before this set ends.'

'Come and meet my parents,' urged Frederica. 'I think we should forget about the duke, do not you? So many grand and beautiful ladies!'

'You are right,' said Maria with a sigh. 'I doubt if he knows we exist.'

'Who is that very beautiful girl over there?' said the duke's friend, Lord Alistair Beaumont. He swung his quizzing-glass on its long chain in Maria's direction.

'Do you find her beautiful, Beau?' asked

the duke, raising his eyebrows. 'I have met her. Name of Kendall. Farouche and noisy and pert. Quite vulgar.'

'Oh, I should never have asked you,' mourned Beau. 'You find fault with every female in Christendom. Well, I am going to find out for myself.'

He moved away and shortly could be seen bowing over Maria and asking her to dance. The duke frowned. Miss Kendall had refused his charitable and magnanimous invitation to dinner. She needed a set-down and it looked as if she was not going to get one. Beau was tall and broad-shouldered, and extremely handsome. Of course, Miss Kendall did look remarkably beautiful in that splendid gown. If one did not know her, then one might make the folly of accounting her a diamond of the first water. He frowned awfully. Why had she refused his invitation to dinner? She was a nobody. He had made it his business to find out about her. No one who was anyone had heard of the Kendalls of Bath. Yes, he had behaved badly by kissing her, but surely his invitation to dinner was apology enough.

Lord Alistair Beaumont, Beau to his friends in particular and to London society in general, was intrigued by Miss Kendall.

She was so graceful, so sensuous, and yet she had a dreamy faraway look in her eyes. Maria was still plotting revenge on the duke, but Beau did not know that.

It was not possible to engage in much conversation during the complicated set of a noisy country dance, although it went on for half an hour, but when the dance was over, he begged to be allowed to take her into supper and was surprised by the slight look of dismay in her eyes and the short hesitation before she politely accepted his invitation. Beau, like his friend the duke, was used to being chased by women rather than having to chase them himself. He did not know Maria had been hoping for an invitation from the duke.

He next asked Frederica to dance. Frederica accepted gracefully. Her last partner had been the village butcher who had trodden on her toes, and they were still aching.

The duke, at last mindful of his duties, invited the vicar's wife to dance, and when that dance was over he moved about the guests seated around the room, talking to first one and then the other.

He found himself growing increasingly annoyed with Miss Kendall. Men were now vying with each other for dances with her, and then he saw Beau moving forward to lead her into supper.

His partner for supper was his own mother. He felt very old and stuffy.

'Who's that fetching gal with Beaumont?' asked his mother, her faded eyes peering across the supper room.

'A Miss Kendall, Mama.'

'Interesting-looking gal. Out of the common way. Might do for Beau. Time he settled down. Kendall? Kendall? Pushy couple of mushrooms accosted me in the Pump Room in Bath. Bragging on about their beautiful daughter and how they were paying a fortune to them Tribble twins to puff her off.'

'The Tribbles, Mama? The sponsors of the difficult and impossible? What is up with Miss Kendall?'

'Don't know,' said his mother vaguely, turning over in her mind all the Bath scandals she had heard. 'Oh, I think I have it. Ain't a virgin. Lost it to Harry Templar at Comfreys' hunt ball. In the pantry, of all places. Wouldn't think there would be enough room.'

The duke leaned back in his chair, a smile curling his lips. So the dewy-fresh and dreamy Miss Kendall was not what she appeared. And to think he had felt guilty for having kissed her.

He hoped for her sake her parents had a great deal of money. Even the famous Tribbles would find it hard to marry off a young girl who had shamefully and openly lost her virginity.

'She told me she was engaged to a ship's captain,' said the duke. 'If she is already engaged, why does she need a Season?'

'Don't ask me,' said his mother. 'Maybe the captain heard the scandal and cried off.'

Beau, the duke noticed, was gazing adoringly at Miss Kendall. His friend would have to be warned. The duke was apt to take care of his friends with the same patronizing kindness as he took care of his tenants. So far he had never done anything to interfere in Beau's life, which was possibly why Beau was one of his very few close friends.

After supper, Maria was surrounded by a crowd of men begging her for the next dance. Beau shrugged ruefully and walked away to join the duke.

'Step aside with me a little,' murmured the duke. 'There is something I must tell you.'

They strolled together out of the assembly room and into the quietness of the hall.

'What is it?' asked Beau lightly. 'You look

deuced serious.'

'I must put you on your guard against Miss Kendall.'

'I think you should stop right there,' said Beau angrily. 'You said she was common and vulgar and she is neither. She is one of the most enchanting girls I have ever met.'

'Mama heard that Miss Kendall lost her virginity in the pantry at the Comfreys' hunt ball. She is being sent to the Tribbles.'

'Fustian! Who are the Tribbles?'

'You are out of touch.'

'I have been travelling abroad, as you know.'

'They are spinster ladies who reside in London and charge a vast sum to bring out so-called difficult girls.'

'I cannot believe you,' said Beau. 'Oh, not about the Tribbles, but about her not being a virgin.'

'I am not in the way of relating vicious slander, and neither is my mother,' said the duke.

'No, I suppose not,' said Beau gloomily.

'Cheer up, my friend. If she is so careless with her favours, perhaps you may have them without marriage.'

Beau shook his head sadly. But when they returned to the ballroom, they arrived on the scene just as Maria had decided to begin to flirt to see if she could attract the duke's attention.

Beau saw the roguish looks she was casting at her partner and his heart sank. Still, she was such a beautiful creature that the least he could do was to get a kiss from her.

But he could not get near Maria for the rest of that evening, she was so besieged by partners.

The ball finished in the small hours with an announcement that the duke's estate workers had diverted the torrent and repaired the road. The travellers would be able to continue their journey.

Beau had been drinking a great deal. He became more determined than ever to see Maria alone.

Maria was sitting at her toilet table and Betty was just about to unpin the silk roses from her hair when there came a scratching at the door and then a note was slid underneath it.

Betty picked it up and gave it to Maria. 'What is it?' asked Miss Spiggs avidly. 'What an odd time to deliver a message.'

Maria swung away from her and quickly read the message: 'Meet me in the coffee room as soon as possible, Beaumont.'

'I must go,' said Maria. 'Miss Sunningdale wants to see me about something. Don't wait up for me, Betty. Both you and Miss Spiggs go to bed.'

She swung a long cloak about her shoulders, made her way down to the coffee room and pushed open the door.

It was empty except for Lord Alistair Beaumont, who was standing, leaning one arm on the mantel and looking down into the embers of the fire.

He swung round as Maria entered.

Maria knew she should not have come, but the prospect that Lord Alistair might mean to propose marriage to her was too big a temptation. She thought of the duke's outraged face when he learned she had enslaved his best friend. That was almost as good a revenge as spurning the duke.

'My darling, I knew you would come,' said Beau. He strode towards her, caught her in his arms and began to kiss her passionately.

Maria struggled and then managed to kick Beau hard on his shin.

He yelped and released her.

'How dare you!' whispered Maria fiercely. She longed to shout and scream, but she knew her very presence alone in the coffee room in the middle of the night with Lord

Alistair would damn her morals, and wondered miserably why she had not thought of such a thing in the first place.

'Don't come the prim miss with me,' laughed Beau. 'I confess your air of innocence had me fooled, but when Berham told me how you gave your favours away in the pantry at the Comfreys' hunt ball, I decided I may as well help myself to your rose-buds.'

'I do not know what you are talking about,' said Maria furiously. 'You are a drunken lecher, sir.'

She darted out of the coffee room and locked the door behind her.

Head held high, she marched up the stairs to her room. She met the Duke of Berham in the passage.

He started to give her a bow and then reeled back, for Maria had swung back her fist and boxed him hard on the ear. She went into her room and closed the door.

He recovered from the shock and was going to hammer on her door and demand an explanation when his mother came along the passage in a billowing night-gown and enormous nightcap.

'Oh, there you are, Rupert,' she said. 'Shall you be returning home tomorrow, or do you plan to go to London directly now the road is clear?'

'I shall be returning home for a couple of days, Mama, and then I shall leave.'

'Very well.' The dowager duchess half-turned away and then turned back and said, 'I have just remembered. It was not the Kendall girl who behaved so disgracefully at that hunt ball. It was Miss Caroline Moray. I really do seem to get things mixed up these days. So sad. A sign of age, I fear.'

She wandered off.

The duke stood for a moment, his face flaming. Beau must have tried something. Damn. He would apologize to her in the morning. He had always prided himself on his courtesy and manners. Never in his life had he behaved so badly to anyone as he had behaved to Maria Kendall. Never before had he related such a damning piece of slanderous gossip about anyone.

Maria did not go to bed. She changed into her travelling clothes and waited by the window for dawn. Then she went downstairs and summoned her servants to bring the carriage around and then went back to her room and roused Miss Spiggs and Betty.

A red sun was glaring across the watery fields as they set out. Maria's heart felt as heavy as lead. The miles crept by. The harness creaked, the joists rattled, and Miss Spiggs snored.

And then out of the gloomy soil of misery, Maria cultivated a splendid dream. Her captain did exist. He was tall and powerful and gallant. She could see him striding into White's in St James's and drawing off one of his gloves and striking the evil duke across the face. The dream moved to Parliament Hill Fields. The spires of London rose through the morning mist as her gallant captain shot the wicked duke right through the heart.

'Forgive me, Miss Kendall,' whispered the duke brokenly just before he breathed his last.

The fantasy was warm and comforting. Maria might have been more comforted if she could have seen what was happening in reality at that moment outside the inn. The duke had told Beau of his mistake and the infuriated Beau had demanded satisfaction. So, stripped to the waist, the two aristocrats were ferociously punching each other around the inn-yard. The landlord was running a betting book and the fight created high excitement in the neighbourhood but was accounted a great disappointment in the end, for the men were so equally matched that they all but punched each other senseless before they were dragged apart.

The ladies, too, were disappointed, for original gossip had it that both men were fighting over some female, but it transpired that Beau had said that the duke's cravat was a disgrace and the duke had taken it as an insult.

Maria had feared the Tribbles would turn out to be stern taskmasters, and therefore her welcome took her aback. Miss Amy Tribble, a tall and commanding figure, hugged her and burst into tears, said she was glad she was safe, and pretty little Miss Effy fluttered about her, reciting a catalogue of all the things that had been done to ensure her comfort. Miss Kendall would find the bed in her room was new and the mattress was stuffed with the best eiderdown. A fire had been lit and if she needed anything she had only to ring.

Maria's eyes filled with grateful tears as she thanked them.

When she had gone upstairs, Effy looked at her sister anxiously. 'We knew the roads were bad, Amy. It is not at all like you to be so overcome.'

'I'll be all right,' said Amy gruffly. 'Don't know what's up with me these days.' And Amy did not. Her emotions seemed to see-saw wildly. Occasionally she was plagued with great flushes of fiery heat but somehow she could not discuss this with her sister. To add to Amy's discomfort, her desire for marriage to Mr Haddon had been manage-able while it remained a simple desire not to remain a spinster. But she had fallen in love with him and there was no one to tell Amy that love in the fifties can be as agonizing and piercing as love in the teens. She did not even know herself that she was deeply in love, for love was supposed to be a happy state, not this terrible yearning to see him and then, when he did come, feeling gauche and desperately inadequate.

'I think we should get shot of that com-panion of hers,' said Effy. 'A sad creature.'

'Yes, don't want her underfoot. Nasty smile and creeping ways,' said Amy roundly.

But getting rid of Miss Spiggs proved to be a difficult task. No sooner was that lady told she was expected to return to Bath the following day than she broke down and wept that no one wanted her, no one would ever want her. Maria's kind heart was touched and she asked leave to keep Miss

Spiggs just for another week; the sisters reluctantly gave their permission.

They regretted their magnanimity when Mr Haddon and Mr Randolph called after dinner. Both gentlemen showed Miss Spiggs every courtesy and Miss Spiggs flirted with them quite appallingly.

Then came a distressing scene. Yvette was called down to the drawing room to meet Maria. Yvette was the resident French dressmaker. To Maria's surprise, she entered carrying a large and healthy rosy-cheeked baby. While the baby was placed on the carpet and Yvette began to tell Maria she would take a look at her wardrobe and see what could be altered, Miss Spiggs quietly asked Effy if Yvette's husband was resident as well and Effy, who was feeling tired and besides had become used to Yvette and the baby, said that Yvette was not married because some wicked French seducer had disappeared after having got her with child.

Miss Spiggs began to shriek that dear Maria could not remain in such a household and appealed to Mr Haddon. Mr Haddon was not allowed to reply because Amy called Miss Spiggs 'a mealy-mouthed, Friday-faced bitch's offspring with a face like a twat' and Miss Spiggs fell on the floor in a spasm and drummed her heels. Maria carefully removed flowers from a vase and tipped the water over Miss Spiggs, who relapsed into sobs.

Effy rang the bell and told her own lady's maid, Baxter, to remove Miss Spiggs, which Baxter, being very strong and powerful, did with great ease.

'I must apologize for my companion,' said Maria, 'but she was not my choice. Still, it must be very hard to cope with genteel poverty and to always be ingratiating.'

'I did not find her ingratiating in the least,' said Amy hotly. 'In fact, she was damned rude. Not that you gentlemen seemed to notice, the way you were hanging around her.'

'I was sorry for her,' said Mr Haddon sternly. 'She is a poor creature' – by which he meant a poor sort of creature, but Amy's jealousy flared up.

'Well, if your fancy is a lady with great fat bosoms shoved up under her chin and a penchant for tight silk gowns, then I have no more to say to you,' Amy lashed out.

Mr Haddon and Amy were both very tall, and Effy and Mr Randolph both small and neat and dainty. Amy and Mr Haddon stood glaring at each other while Mr Randolph and Effy fluttered about them in a useless kind of way.

Yvette picked up baby George and said she would go to Maria's room and look at her gowns, and Maria eagerly said she would go with her.

Amy half-turned to follow them, but Mr Haddon said quietly, 'No, Miss Amy. At this moment Yvette is setting a better example in manners and courtesy than you.'

'Ho!' said Amy. 'It was not I who screamed out in shock over Yvette's bastard but your latest fancy, sirrah.'

'What is up with you, woman?' shouted Mr Haddon. 'You have lost your wits. You may stay, Randolph, but I have had just as much of this company as I am going to take this evening.'

Amy stood, her large hands hanging at her sides as Mr Haddon, that normally quiet and polite gentleman, stormed his way out. Mr Randolph cleared his throat nervously. 'I must say goodbye as well,' he said.

Effy made a bleating sound of protest, but Mr Randolph almost ran from the room.

Mr Randolph caught up with his friend at the corner of Holles Street. 'Come along,' he said. 'Let's go to the club. I've had enough of females for one night.'

'But you know,' said Mr Haddon as he fell

into step beside Mr Randolph, 'that female did have a face like a twat.' And then he began to giggle in a most unmanly way.

3

Youth had been a habit of hers for so long that she could not part with it.

Rudyard Kipling

It was unfortunate for Amy that Mr Haddon contracted a severe cold after that noisy argument. He did send a servant around to Holles Street with a letter explaining his illness, but the servant dropped the letter by mistake on the way there and, being new in Mr Haddon's household, was too fearful of losing his job to tell the truth. Mr Randolph had gone off to see friends in the country on the comfortable assumption that Mr Haddon would be around to explain his absence, and so it was that the two Tribble sisters felt sadly neglected and Effy blamed Amy and Amy blamed herself.

Still, they were mindful of their duties and

set about behaving like paragon duennas to remove any unfortunate first impressions that Miss Maria Kendall might have been given of them. After four days of Miss Spiggs, both sisters set about dispatching that lady back to Bath so firmly and so determinedly that she could find nothing left to make her stay longer.

Maria watched her go with a sigh of relief. She was enjoying the Tribble household. She had only been out for short drives with Effy. Most of her time was taken up with pinnings and fittings as Yvette remodelled her wardrobe while baby George played and gurgled at their feet.

Amy's sensitivities were still raw. She felt she should write to Mr Haddon, begging forgiveness, but a stiff-necked pride would not let her do so. Effy was still enjoying Amy's guilt and so did not write either. Although Effy preferred Mr Randolph, it would be a sweeter victory to snatch Mr Haddon from her sister, and so the longer the couple remained estranged, the better. It was the first time Effy had even admitted to herself that the nabob's feelings towards Amy might be a trifle warmer than they were towards herself.

Effy and Maria had gone out driving one

fine afternoon and Amy was left to her gloomy thoughts when the Duke of Berham was announced.

She told Harris, the butler, to send him up to the drawing room.

Now, when she was miserable, Amy regressed back to the days of her poverty and liked to soothe her spirits by doing housework. She had been engaged in cleaning out closets, and her hair was tied up in a scarf and she was wearing an old apron.

The Duke of Berham entered. His glance rested briefly on Amy and slid away.

'Please be seated, your grace,' said Amy.

'No, thank you,' said the duke haughtily. 'I shall wait until your mistress arrives.'

His gaze contemptuously took in the scarf and apron.

Amy blushed furiously. 'I am Miss Amy Tribble,' she said crossly.

'Indeed!' the duke sat down. 'I had hoped to see Miss Kendall.'

'Miss Kendall is out driving. I was not aware you were acquainted with her.'

The duke looked silently at Amy. If Miss Kendall had not troubled to tell this odd chaperone of the unfortunate happenings at the inn, then perhaps he should let sleeping dogs lie. He was not interested in Miss Kendall, and to pursue the matter might raise false hopes. The duke was used to being pursued.

He rose and bowed. 'I am sure Miss Kendall will not remember me. I should not have called. Please do not tell her of my visit. It is of no consequence.'

His glacial manner, his air of consequence, and the lurking contempt in those eyes of his made Amy hate him with a passion.

'I am sure you can see yourself out,' she said, and before he had even left the room, she had seized a feather duster and was busily cleaning gleaming furniture without a single speck of dust on it.

Amy decided to put the duke's visit out of her mind. Maria Kendall was of too low an order to aspire to a duke.

After Amy had finished cleaning, she decided to go for a ride in the Park and went and changed into her riding costume.

She was cantering through the Park when she saw the duke approaching in his carriage. Feeling she had not behaved very well, and, after all, a duke was a duke, Amy decided to speak to him. She moved alongside his carriage and cried, 'Good day.'

It never dawned on Amy that the duke would not recognize her, that Yvette's creation of smart blue velvet riding dress and blue velvet hat would make her look a different person entirely from the angry woman with her hair tied up in a scarf. The duke was used to being hailed by encroaching people to whom he had not even been introduced. He slightly raised his thin eyebrows, clicked his tongue at his horses, and bowled away at a smart pace. It was the cut direct. Amy's face flamed.

The Tribbles, even in their poorest days, had never been cut by anyone. They were *bon ton.*

Amy was furious. She returned to Holles Street, now determined to find out what Maria knew of the duke.

Effy had gone to lie down. Amy found Maria in her room. She was sitting in a chair by the window, dreamily staring at nothing.

'The Duke of Berham called when you were out,' said Amy.

To her surprise, tears started to Maria's eyes and she covered her face with her hands. 'Dreadful man,' she mumbled incoherently. 'I could kill him!'

Amy snatched Maria's hands away from her face and demanded, 'What is the matter? What has he done?'

Maria controlled herself with an effort. The

duke may have behaved badly, but she felt sure she had brought some of the trouble on herself by her own behaviour. She was not afraid of Amy, cleverly recognizing the sympathetic and soft-hearted soul which lurked under Amy's hard mannish exterior. And so she told her everything. About the kiss, about the ball, about her own fantasy of humiliating him and her lie about her fiancé, about how Lord Beaumont had been told by the duke that she had already lost her virginity. 'I even told him my fiancé, Captain Jack Free-mantle, would call him out,' said Maria.

It was an age when not very many women survived into their fifties and there was no one to tell Amy that occasionally in the lives of women of a certain age, there could be times when they were not quite sane. Amy had been completely thrown off balance by what she saw as Mr Haddon's rejection of her. The duke's snub had added fuel to her temporary insanity. She forgot about Maria's fantasizing and did not realise that here was surely a good opportunity to point out the folly of living in a dream-world. She merely patted Maria on the hand and said, 'Leave things to me. You shall have your revenge.'

Maria, who was impressed by Amy's bold manner and standing in London society, assumed Amy would send for the duke and read him the lecture he deserved. Had she known what Amy was planning, she would have been horrified.

Amy was going to challenge the duke to a duel.

The fact that she had once masqueraded as a man to break up a duel between Mr Haddon and a fribble called Callaghan, and had been instantly recognized as Miss Amy Tribble by Mr Haddon, did not deter her. She simply thought that on that occasion she had not taken enough pains over her disguise.

The following day, she went to a naval outfitters and ordered a sea captain's uniform. She told them it was for a fancy dress ball and urged them to make haste. She then sent for the hairdresser and told him she wanted one of the new fashionable crops and felt quite weepy as her heavy iron-grey locks were shorn, since Amy considered her long hair the only feminine attribute she had possessed. While Amy plotted and planned, Effy and Maria went on calls, went shopping, went to Gunter's for ices, and remained unaware of the volcano of revenge that was smouldering inside Miss Amy Tribble.

Maria was to make her début in two

weeks' time at a grand ball given by Lord and Lady Livingstone. Amy knew the social calendar inside out and knew at which functions before then she would be likely to meet the Duke of Berham. There was to be a concert given at the home of Mrs Darby, and all the cream of society was expected to be there. Amy called on Mrs Darby and told her that a dashing and handsome sea captain, a Mr Jack Freemantle, who was distantly related to her, would be in London and longed for the civilizing sounds of good music. Much intrigued, Mrs Darby offered an invitation to the captain. Amy said that neither she nor Effy could attend because they had to school their latest charge and bring her up to the mark for her début.

With the invitation secure in her reticule, she next called again on the outfitters for a final fitting. The naval costume would be ready in time for Mrs Darby's concert.

The naval outfitters had been told no expense was to be spared, and thinking that the captain's costume was meant for a fancy dress ball, they had added a great deal more gold embellishment to it than a sea captain would ever dare to wear.

Amy's next worry was how to make her escape from home dressed as a naval captain on the eve of the concert. She hired a dancing master to come round that evening to instruct Maria in the steps of the waltz, although Maria protested she knew the steps very well. Amy then pleaded the headache and begged Effy to play the piano for the dancing lesson. As soon as she heard the first chord of the waltz sounding from below, Amy locked herself in her room and pomaded and powdered her new short hair. Then she donned the naval uniform: short blue dress jacket with brass buttons and gold epaulettes, and medal ribbons worn over a white waistcoat. White knee breeches, white silk stockings and black leather slippers completed the ensemble. She looked doubtfully at the hat before putting it on. It was surely an admiral's hat. She shrugged. She would not be wearing it when she challenged the duke to a duel.

She tugged down her dress jacket and looked at herself in the mirror. A distinguished tall slim naval man with a harsh face stared back. Amy blinked away sudden tears. She had always longed to be a pretty woman, but her mirror showed her it would have been better for her to have been born a man. She then picked up a small trunk into which she had packed the masculine clothes for previous masquerades and fancy dress parties, hoisted it onto her shoulder, and crept quietly down the stairs and let herself out, after leaving a note on the hall table in which she said she had gone off to visit a friend in the country. She then took a hack to Limmer's Hotel, where she had already booked a room under the name of Captain Freemantle. It was traditional for seconds in a duel to call and try to talk the antagonist out of it, and she could hardly have them calling at Holles Street. Not once did she stop to think that perhaps she might have run mad. Amy felt she had a purpose in life. It was not only the duke she would be getting even with but all the world of men who made life so hard and lonely for unwanted spinsters.

When she arrived at Mrs Darby's concert, she was glad she had told that lady that the captain was a relative of the Tribbles, for Mrs Darby kept exclaiming over the captain's resemblance to Miss Amy.

The duke was not there. Amy's heart sank. She sat as wooden-faced as any sailor while the concert went on and on. At last it was over and supper was announced. Amy rose and turned about and then she saw the duke standing at the back of the concert room talking to a handsome man.

Amy took a deep breath and drew off her gloves. Eyes fixed on the duke and ignoring everyone else, she marched up to him.

She struck him sharply across the cheek with her gloves and said in a harsh voice, 'I am Captain Jack Freemantle of His Majesty's Navy. You insulted my fiancée and I demand satisfaction. Name your seconds.'

And as she looked into the Duke of Berham's cold eyes, Amy realised for the first time that he would probably kill her.

Mr Haddon was not usually given over to self-pity. But he felt neglected and unloved. Any time he had been indisposed before, the Tribble sisters had sent messages and baskets of fruit. Not even a letter had arrived. He felt hot and feverish and could not sleep. It was two nights after Mrs Darby's party. He had been invited but had been too unwell to go. He had read an item in his newspaper that morning that a sensation had been caused at the concert by a certain captain who had challenged the Duke of B. to a duel. Mr Haddon was not interested enough to wonder which duke this could be. At last, he fell into an uneasy sleep from which he wakened at dawn, feeling weak but much better. His fever had abated. He heard a horse's hooves in the street below. Someone had reined in at his door. He looked at the clock. Five-thirty in the morning. He climbed from bed, went to the window and leaned out. A tall figure in naval dress was stooping to slide a letter under his door. The figure straightened up and mounted the horse. Mr Haddon stared. There was something in the manner and bearing that reminded him forcibly of Amy.

He went downstairs, picked up the letter and opened it. In the pale dawn light coming through the fanlight over the door he read the first line – 'Last Will and Testament of Amy Tribble.'

It all rushed into his mind at once – the naval captain who looked so much like Amy, that duel at the concert, how Amy had once before dressed up as a man.

His heart began to hammer. He shouted and shouted for his servants while all the while he wondered where the duel would be. Chalk Farm? Parliament Hill Fields? Hyde Park?

By the time he had mounted his horse, he had decided Chalk Farm was the safest bet.

Amy's seconds were two noisy bucks from Limmer's Hotel who had readily agreed to stand for her. Amy had already received visits from the duke's seconds, Lord Alistair Beaumont and a Mr Henry Wainwright. Beau had explained how the duke had made the mistake about Miss Kendall's reputation and had begged the 'captain' to call off the duel. But the madness was still in Amy and she was determined to go through with it.

But it was a very shaky and feminine and weak Amy who stood on Parliament Hill Fields as the sun rose and the sleepy birds began to twitter in the trees. The first buds were just beginning to uncurl and the air was sweet and fresh. It was a morning to be alive – to stay alive, thought Amy gloomily.

But she really felt she had nothing to live for. Mr Haddon had deserted her, as so many men had deserted her in the past. Her love for him had enveloped her like a warm blanket. Now it had been snatched away, leaving her soul shivering and naked in a hostile world, a world which many of her friends had already left.

The duke arrived. He was dressed in black, with the lapels of his coat folded over his cravat so as to leave the least target for his opponent. Amy was still wearing that naval dress and her brass buttons winked in the sunlight.

The surgeon arrived and took up his position. The antagonists each selected a long duelling pistol.

Then the duke and Amy stood back to back and began to pace away from each other.

Mr Haddon, having found no sign of a duel at Chalk Farm, was now riding hell for leather to Parliament Hill Fields.

The Duke of Berham felt highly annoyed by the whole proceedings. He wondered which part of the captain's anatomy he should put a ball through. He was an expert shot. He hoped vaguely the captain was not equally good but did not feel very much concerned. The London Season had proved a monstrous bore and this duel was an added irritation.

'Ten,' he counted and swung about and took careful aim.

Mr Haddon rode onto the duelling field at the same time as the shots were fired and saw the captain fall like a stone.

The duke turned away and handed his pistol to Beau and said, 'Breakfast, I think. I am sharp set.'

'What about the other fellow?' demanded Beau hotly. 'You've killed him.'

'Not I. I carefully put a ball through the fleshy part of his arm.'

'You're a cold devil,' said Beau. 'I'm going

to make sure just the same.'

Mr Wainwright and Amy's seconds were hotly arguing over bets in a corner of the field.

'Is she dead?' whispered Mr Haddon, kneeling beside the surgeon. The surgeon was cutting away Amy's jacket. 'She?' he asked. 'You mean he, sir.' Then his eyebrows rose in amazement as his probing fingers felt the softness of Amy's bosom.

The duke was just strolling away, arm in arm with Beau, when the surgeon's shout stopped him. 'This is a woman, your grace.'

'Will she live?' cried Mr Haddon.

'Yes, yes,' said the surgeon testily. 'The ball went clean through the fleshy part of her arm.'

'What is all this?' snapped the duke. 'What do you mean, a woman?'

'I fear you have shot Miss Amy Tribble,' said Mr Haddon. The surgeon was efficiently binding up the wound. Mr Haddon took out a flask of brandy and forced it between Amy's pale lips.

'What's she doing masquerading as a captain and challenging me to a duel?' demanded the duke. 'Will no one answer me?'

'I think the only person who can give you any explanation is Miss Amy herself,' said Mr

Haddon as Amy choked on the brandy and her eyes fluttered open. She looked up at Mr Haddon and sighed, 'Am I in Heaven?' she whispered.

The duke wondered how he could ever have mistaken Amy for a man when he saw that look.

'No, Miss Amy,' said Mr Haddon bracingly. 'You have a flesh wound. Goodness, does Miss Effy know of this?'

'No. No one must know,' said Amy brokenly. 'Scandal. Get rid of my seconds. Couple of fellows from Limmer's. Mustn't know the truth.'

'See to it, Beau,' said the duke, 'and get rid of Wainwright as well. Do you think they heard that shout that she was a woman?'

'No,' said the surgeon. 'Mr Wainwright and the others were arguing about something. I am sure they did not hear.'

While Beau went off, Mr Haddon said to the duke, 'We must get her somewhere she can change out of these clothes.'

The duke frowned impatiently. He had been thoroughly shocked for the first time in his life. All he wanted to do was get the disgraceful Amy out of public view before a major scandal broke about his ears.

'Help her to my carriage,' he said. 'We will

take her to my town house. My mother is in residence.'

Mr Haddon and Beau supported Amy to the duke's carriage. Amy was more distressed by what she had done than by the pain from her throbbing wound. Surely there was no way such a scandal could be hushed up.

As soon as they were in the carriage, Beau began to ask questions, but the duke interrupted him, saying that there would be time enough for questions when they had reached home.

Home was the Berham town house, a large double-fronted building in Cavendish Square. The duke led the party into the library on the ground floor and asked the butler to fetch the dowager duchess.

The butler was well trained. Not by one flicker of surprise did his face display that carrying a wounded captain into the ducal library was in any way out of the ordinary.

The dowager duchess entered, leaning on a silver-topped ebony cane. She sat down and looked curiously at the odd group. 'What's that woman doing dressed as a sea captain?' she asked, looking at Amy.

'I will explain,' said the duke wearily, and he proceeded to do just that, leaving nothing out, from his kissing of Maria to the

76

fight with Beau in the inn courtyard to the duel with Miss Amy Tribble.

'I do not understand it,' said the dowager duchess when he had finished. 'I do not understand *you*, Rupert. I misled you with a scurrilous piece of gossip and for that I am sorry. But when did you ever before behave so badly? And what on earth persuaded you, Miss Tribble, to dress up as a man and challenge my son to a duel?'

'Because I am run mad,' said Amy wanly.

'I think we may well be able to keep it all quiet,' went on the duke's mother. 'Miss Tribble may rest up here until she is strong enough to go home. But the scandal is not my main concern. My chief worry is why you, my son, commandeered a young lady's room and private parlour in that high-handed manner, why you kissed her as if she were a serving wench, and why you then saw fit to make matters worse by trying to call on her. Did he see her, Miss Tribble?'

'No,' said Amy. 'He was rude to me and then he cut me in the Park. I thought he needed to be taught a lesson. Unfortunately it was I who needed to be taught a lesson. I am lucky to be alive.'

'I am a very good shot,' said the duke. 'I could have easily killed you had I wanted to.'

'I think you had better marry this Miss Kendall,' said the dowager duchess.

There was a shocked silence. 'I see no reason for that, Mama,' said the duke stiffly.

The duchess leaned forward, her chin on the knob of her cane, and looked up at her son. 'If you do not marry the girl, then I shall feel obliged to talk about the duel and about your behaviour.'

Amy groaned faintly and Mr Haddon said sharply, 'Can we not discuss this later? Miss Amy is ill.'

'Ring the bell over there and we'll get her put to bed,' said the dowager duchess. 'Take yourself off, Beau, and keep quiet, do you hear? You stay here with me, Rupert. We have much to discuss.'

When mother and son were finally alone, the duke said quietly, 'Now, Mama, what has come over you? I am not going to marry a pert nobody who has been sent to those eccentric Tribbles for schooling – although what sort of manners she is supposed to learn in a house where one of her chaperones dresses as a man and goes about fighting duels, I do not know. She told me some rubbish about being engaged to a sea captain, and no doubt Miss Tribble decided to act out the lie.'

'They have behaved badly, yes, and that should exonerate you – but think. You have become stuffy and high-handed and quite middle-aged in your manner, Rupert. This girl is the first one who has made you behave out of character. I saw her at that ball. Vastly fetching. Her parents are vulgar in the extreme, but rich, very rich, and we Berhams would not have stayed in our position of power if we had gone about marrying for love. You do not suppose for a minute that your father was in love with me? You show no signs of falling in love with anyone other than yourself, and so you may as well settle for an arranged marriage. I have a mind to see the succession secured before I die.'

'Mama, I would do much to please you, but marry that oddity, Maria Kendall, I will most certainly not.'

His mother looked mulish. 'Then I shall talk.'

'And I shall talk, too, and say that age has finally addled your brains.'

His mother looked at him mournfully. Tears welled up in her eyes and rolled down her withered cheeks.

He turned away in embarrassment. He could not remember seeing his mother cry before.

'Dry your eyes,' he said harshly.

His mother's plaintive voice sounded in his ears. 'She would be perfect for you. She is young and can be trained.'

'I shall marry a woman who will grace my rank,' he said over his shoulder.

'Who?' demanded his mother with a choked sob.

He started pacing up and down. 'I shall make amends, Mama,' he said. 'It is her début. I shall dance with her and pay her particular attention. But I cannot marry her. And now, if you will excuse me, I shall go and see how Miss Amy is faring.'

After he had left, the dowager duchess dried her eyes, kicked a footstool across the room, and then rang the bell. 'Get Jessey here,' she ordered. Mr Jessey was the ducal secretary.

When he entered, the duchess said, 'I have good news for you, Mr Jessey. My son is to be married. Take down the details and make sure the announcement appears in every newspaper in the morning.'

The duke found Amy had changed into one of his mother's gowns and was insisting on going home. Weakly, she said she was sorry, she would never breathe a word of the duel, that Effy and Maria believed her to be in the country.

'And how shall you explain the wound?' asked Mr Haddon.

'Carriage accident or highwaymen,' said Amy. 'Oh, Mr Haddon, I am so ashamed of myself, I do not know what to do.'

Mr Haddon thought Amy Tribble had every reason to be thoroughly ashamed of herself and opened his mouth to say so but instead found himself saying, 'Now, now, my beautiful and gallant lady. This is not like you.'

At his words, Amy felt strong and well. She felt she could fight any battle that lay ahead. 'I am very sorry, your grace,' said Amy.

'Your apology is accepted,' he replied. 'But a word of caution. Miss Kendall comes from an unfortunate background and cannot hope to make a dazzling match. You must not encourage either farouche behaviour or ambitious hopes. I have a few friends in the City among the professional and merchant class who would be eminently suitable. You may call on me for help.'

Amy said nothing. Mr Haddon found himself becoming highly irritated with the duke. Under the circumstances, it was a generous offer. But there was something cold-blooded and patronizing about it.

'I am sure the Misses Tribble are experi-enced enough to find suitors for their charge without your help,' he said haughtily. 'Miss Amy, if you really feel strong enough to leave, then I think we should go now.'

The duke, looking at Mr Haddon, was sharply reminded of one of his former tutors who had said, 'A gentleman should be easy and gracious in his manner with all ranks. It is a talent you lack.'

He was glad to see them go. He could now put the whole matter out of his mind.

Effy was alarmed when the wounded Amy arrived home. Mr Haddon told her soothingly that Amy had been shot by highwaymen on her road home. 'On the road home from *where?*' demanded Effy. 'Who do we know in the country, Amy? Who did you visit?'

'Don't plague me with questions,' growled Amy. 'I'm going to bed.'

Effy wanted to talk to Mr Haddon about Maria, but Mr Haddon promptly took his leave. Effy was worried. She had taken Maria out on calls and there was no denying the girl had behaved just as she ought except she did not seem to be *there*. Her eyes held a vague dreamy look and she answered all questions politely but with an air of abstraction.

Baxter, the Tribbles' lady's maid, had told Maria that the Duke of Berham had called. Miss Effy, said Baxter, had been puzzled by the visit and had wondered why Miss Amy had said nothing about it, not realizing Amy had already done so. Maria insisted she did not know what had prompted his grace to call on her. She was sure Amy's absence had something to do with the revenge on the duke Amy had promised and felt it would be better to remain silent on the subject until Amy returned.

Maria meanwhile was wrapped in dreams of spurning the duke. He always proposed, she always refused and he crawled away in shame taking his broken heart with him. This was the best dream Maria had had in a long time and she nourished it and embroidered it until in her mind's eye the duke became older-looking, with a certain seedy grandeur about him as befitting a crumbling aristocrat.

She was disappointed when Amy refused to see her but accepted it was because Amy had been shot by a highwayman. Maria thought Amy a most romantic figure.

Maria always woke early in the morning because in Bath her parents always rose late and she was used to treasuring the peace of the mornings. The morning after Amy's return was no exception.

Effy had given Maria a list of eligibles and had told her to check the engagements in the newspapers and mark off any possibles who had already been snatched up.

Maria read all the advertisements first. There was a Miss Thomas of Chancery Lane advertising ready-made dresses 'to fit all sizes', and F. Newbery and Sons were offering every kind of remedy from Dr James's Powders to Convulsion Pills. A gentleman who had left a brown pelisse coat lined with fur in a hackney chariot was promising three guineas for its return. She turned to the social news and began to read about a grand party that had been illuminated with hundreds of Chinese lamps when her eye was caught by a small announcement farther down the page. She was sure she had seen the name Kendall. But then Kendall was quite an ordinary name.

And then the announcement seemed to scream at her that there was to be a forthcoming marriage between His Grace, The Duke of Berham, and Miss Maria Kendall, only daughter of Mr and Mrs Kendall of Bath. The announcement was very short, the duke's secretary having known only what he had gleaned from the dowager duchess, who did not know whether Maria was the Kendalls' only child, but had simply assumed that if such vulgar persons were paying the Tribbles' costly bill, then it stood to reason Maria must be their sole offspring.

Maria slowly put down the paper and thought hard. The duke had kissed her. It now seemed as if that kiss had been the kiss of a man driven by passion rather than an insulting gesture from an enraged aristocrat. Her feelings softened towards the duke. It was an outrageous thing to do, but he must have felt it was the only way he could secure her. She knew from the social columns that his mother was staying with him at the ducal town house; therefore there would be no scandal in her visiting him. She would tell him gently she could never marry him. At the back of Maria's brain there was a sort of stern older sister always monitoring her folly. This voice told her that the advertisement was nothing more than an embarrassing mistake, that the duke would be furious, and that she should leave the handling of the matter to the Tribbles. But the younger Maria, who had learned to live in dreams to escape the harsh reality of her parents' pushing vulgarity and bullying, would not listen to that voice of reason.

She did not ring for her maid but dressed herself carefully in an outfit Yvette had created for her. It consisted of a cambric high gown covered with a Spanish robe of pea-green muslin worn with a winged mob-cap of white crepe under a beehive bonnet of moss straw, Limerick gloves, and green kid Spanish slippers.

She went downstairs and told a footman to fetch her a chair, for it was raining lightly outside and she did not want her dress soiled by entering a hackney carriage from the muddy street.

The footman wondered whether he should ask her where she was going, for it was odd that miss did not have her maid with her, but felt such a question might be considered impertinent.

When two Irish chairmen entered the hall carrying the sedan chair on its long poles, the footman listened to see if he could hear where Miss Kendall was going, but she told the chairmen she would give them directions once they were outside.

She was borne at a great rate through the rainy streets as her bearers ran along the pavements shouting, 'Make way!' and showing every sign of being prepared to knock anyone who did not heed their warning into the kennel.

They carried their burden straight into the main hall of the duke's town house in Cavendish Square. Self-conscious under the eyes of the duke's stern butler and a row of liveried footmen, Maria paid off the chairmen and presented her card.

She was led into a library and told to wait. Above the library fireplace was a portrait of the duke's father. He had a look of surprise on his painted face as if wondering what such a common interloper as Maria Kendall was doing calling on his son.

Then the door to the library was held open again by the butler and the Duke of Berham walked in.

4

I have misus'd the king's press damnably.

William Shakespeare

Here was not the faded aristocrat of Maria's recent imaginings but a handsome, virile man. His thick fair hair was cut in the Brutus crop and his coat of biscuit-coloured super-fine was moulded to his powerful shoulders.

He made Maria a low bow, insolent in its court depth and elaboration. 'Miss Kendall,' he said. 'I am indeed honoured. What brings you here?'

He felt sure he knew what had brought her. She had come to apologize for her lies, which had forced Amy Tribble to act as Captain Jack Freemantle.

Maria did not answer immediately. She was gazing at him searchingly. She knew now that whatever had prompted the duke to insert that announcement in the newspapers, it was not passion.

'May I sit down, your grace?' she asked after a long silence.

He ushered her into a chair and then sat down opposite her.

'I was shocked to see the announcement of our forthcoming marriage in the papers this morning,' said Maria. The duke went very still.

'I have not seen the papers yet,' he said. 'You are come early. If there is such an announcement, be assured that mad Amy Tribble put it there. I shall consult my lawyers.' He rang the bell. When the butler answered, he asked him to send Mr Jessey immediately.

'My secretary shall send another notice, publicly stating I have been the victim of a wicked trick,' said the duke icily.

Maria sat frozen with dismay. Was this how Amy had planned to get revenge?

Mr Jessey entered. 'There is an announcement in the newspapers this morning,' began the duke, 'to the effect that I am to wed Miss Kendall.'

'I hope I had all the facts correct,' said Mr Jessey earnestly. 'I wished to consult you on the matter, but her grace said you did not wish to be troubled with it.'

'Her grace? My *mother?* Surely you must be mistaken.'

'No, your grace, I was instructed to place that announcement in all the newspapers.'

'Where is her grace?'

'She has gone to stay with Lady Humphrey at Cheltenham,' said Mr Jessey. 'Did her grace not tell you of this?'

The duke shook his head in bewilderment. Then he said, 'That will be all, Mr Jessey. But do not leave the house. I may need you shortly.'

When the secretary had left, the duke said savagely, 'All women ought to be locked up when they reach the age of forty-five. First Amy Tribble challenges me to a duel, and now my own mother has set out to make me a laughing-stock.'

'A duel?' asked Maria. 'What duel? Is that why Miss Amy is wounded?'

'So you do not know. You amaze me. Miss Amy decided to act the part of that figment of your imagination, Captain Jack Freemantle. She dressed the part and challenged me to a duel. Thinking her a man, I put a ball through her arm.'

'Oh, how brave of her!' cried Maria. 'How very brave.'

He leaned forward and said in measured tones, 'I think the reason I have never married is because I think women are all mad. Are you not shocked that a seemingly respectable spinster should behave in such a scandalous way? Or did you pay her to do it?'

'I told her about those scurrilous lies you had been circulating about me,' said Maria, her eyes flashing. 'I had no man to defend me. Miss Amy said she would see I got my revenge and I thought she meant to call on you and read you the riot act.'

'I apologize to you most sincerely for having been misled as to your character by my own mother,' he said stiffly. 'I am prepared to make amends. My consequence in society is considerable and I shall make it my duty to stand up with you for a few dances and take you driving in the Park.'

'How kind,' said Maria sarcastically. 'Let me tell you, you great lumpkin, I do not want you or your consequence.'

He leaned back in his chair and surveyed her curiously from under his heavy eyelids. 'You do not?' he asked. 'My rank, my favour, and my title do not interest you?'

'Not in the slightest, your grace. I will leave you to repair the damage your mother has done. I only hope the notice in the newspapers explaining the mistake appears before my delighted parents decide to journey to Town, for if they set off immediately today after reading about the forthcoming marriage and then find it is all a mistake when they arrive, they will blame me for the cancellation and I have a mind not to be beaten.'

'Do they beat you much?'

'Yes,' said Maria curtly.

'Why?'

'Why? Because I am not interested in the suitors they find for me. My failure to provide them with an entrée to society makes them very angry.'

He sat for a moment, studying her. He

noticed the clear skin and beautiful eyes and the soft swell of her bosom. He vividly remembered the feel of her lips.

He closed his eyes and thought hard. He would have to marry sooner or later, and he was tired of Season after Season. Maria Kendall was young and pretty and not unamusing. He could do worse. If he married her, he would get the heir he needed and the succession would be ensured. She would get her freedom from those parents who appeared to treat her very harshly, although he was sure her story of beatings was a wild exaggeration.

'As you appear to be settling down to sleep,' remarked Maria acidly, 'I may as well take my leave. I should not be here when your mother is absent.'

His eyes flew open. 'I have two aunts somewhere about, and a housekeeper,' he said. 'Your reputation is safe.'

'In any case, I must leave,' said Maria, getting to her feet.

He rose as well and stood looking down at her.

'I have a proposition to make to you, Miss Kendall,' he said, taking her hand.

She snatched her hand away and glared up at him, a high colour mantling her cheeks.

'Don't you *dare* suggest I become your

mistress,' she said.

'On the contrary. I suggest it might suit us both to let the engagement stand.'

Now was Maria's chance to spurn him, but the tone of voice had been cool and practical.

'Why?' she asked weakly.

'I need to get married sometime. I would be giving you a freedom you cannot enjoy as a single lady. As my duchess you would have great social power.'

'I am not interested in social power,' said Maria almost tearfully, thinking of all her rosy dreams of love.

'Nonetheless, you would be your own mistress. You may lead your own life after we are married. Your main duty will be to present me with a son. After that, you may do as you please.'

'May I sit down?' asked Maria. He helped her to a chair.

She sat and rested her head on her hand. What if this very expensive Season came and went and she did not find someone to love? Her parents would never forgive her. Her life would return to that old hell of nagging and bullying. She had a chance of becoming the Duchess of Berham. She would go to court, be presented to the Queen and the Prince

Regent. She would be a failure, a disgrace, no more in the eyes of her parents. Freedom, he had promised. Freedom to have friends, freedom to dream, freedom to read all the books she wanted. And the Tribble sisters, of whom she had become so very fond, would have a great success. Their charge engaged to a duke before she had even made her début!

If he had said something, if he had interrupted her thoughts, she might have refused him. But he sat down again and waited quietly.

After a time, when she did not speak, he found himself becoming irritated and anxious. What was up with the girl? Any other woman in the land would have jumped at such an opportunity.

At last she raised those fine eyes of hers and looked at him. There was a trace of sadness in them as she said quietly, 'Very well. I accept.'

'You have made me the happiest of men,' he replied politely.

'I doubt that,' said Maria with a sudden gurgle of laughter. 'You look as if you have just successfully bid for a horse.'

'My dear Miss Kendall, I am not entirely without romance in my soul.'

'I think you are,' sighed Maria. 'But you

have offered me freedom and what a beautiful word that is.' Her face clouded over.

'Now what is wrong?' he asked gently.

'I assume you will be travelling to Bath to ask my parents' permission?'

'Of course.'

'You have never met my parents. They may come as a shock to you.'

'I am not high in the instep. It is you I plan to marry, not your parents.'

Maria shook her head. 'You are very proud. I will make you a promise. If, after meeting my parents, you decide not to marry me, I shall understand.'

'I find it distressing in you that you are obviously ashamed of your parents and yet you call *me* proud.'

'Make no mistake about it, I love my parents because they are my parents and their harsh treatment of me is prompted in part by wishing the best for me, but they do disaffect people. Please, your grace, send them an express warning them of your arrival or they will set out for London, and, please, see if I can be married from the Tribbles' home.'

'You are fond of those oddities?'

'The Tribbles? Yes. Very. They are kind and funny and generous.'

'And quite mad,' he said. 'I feel they have

done nothing to earn this social success.'

'When you speak like that,' said Maria, 'I am afraid I might be in danger of taking you in dislike.'

He looked at her in genuine surprise. Dukes were never disliked.

'I shall take you back to the Tribbles,' he said, putting down her last remark to nervousness.

The house in Holles Street was in an uproar when they arrived. Amy was lying on a sofa in the drawing room, wrapped in a quilted banyan and with a turban on her shorn locks. Effy was walking up and down, her many gauze scarves floating about her. Mr Haddon was studying that announcement in *The Morning Post* through a quizzing-glass, and Mr Randolph was sipping tea, trying to look helpful and wondering whether eating one of the delicious cakes on the plate in front of him would show signs of a lack of sensibility.

'It's some mad, cruel joke,' said Effy again. 'Someone is trying to ruin us. And where is Maria?'

'Her parents, I gather,' said Mr Haddon, 'sent her to you in part to cure her of dreaming. Could she not have decided in her dreams that this duke was in love with her and put these advertisements in herself?'

Amy looked stricken. It was beginning to sound like the sort of thing Maria *would* do.

And then Harris announced the arrival of the Duke of Berham and Miss Kendall. Helped by Mr Haddon, Amy struggled upright as the couple entered.

Holding Maria's hand, the duke said, 'You may congratulate me, ladies, gentlemen. We are to be wed.'

There was a stunned silence. What have I done? thought Maria miserably. The hand holding her own was strong and firm and somehow possessive.

Effy fluttered around delightedly on one side of the couple and Mr Randolph did a sort of excited dance step on the other. Mr Haddon looked startled. Amy's shrewd eyes searched Maria's face.

The duke explained how his mother had had the notice inserted for some mischievous reason. Miss Kendall had called on him and they had both decided to go along with the engagement.

Amy was worried. She was sure it was her own folly that had precipitated this engagement. It was a marvellous coup. London society must be talking of little else. She and

Effy would be besieged with offers. But Amy thought Maria was much too young in every way for the duke. She was immature and dreamy. The duke was arrogant and sophisticated. But then could something not be done for Maria? She and Effy were supposed to school their charges and overcome all difficulties.

The duke was saying, Amy realized, that he was going to Bath to ask Mr and Mrs Kendall for their permission. Amy let out a slow breath. Once the haughty duke had met the Kendalls, then the marriage would be off. No man as proud as the duke would be able to tolerate having such in-laws.

Maria began to feel all her fears ebb away as Effy fussed about her and wished her well. Her parents would be proud of her at last.

It would be a splendid wedding. Her mind floated away on a vision of white Brussels lace and clanging church bells.

At last, when the duke, Mr Haddon and Mr Randolph had left and Effy had run upstairs to tell Yvette the glad news, Amy said quietly, 'Come and sit by me, Maria.'

Maria did as she was bid. 'I am most grateful to you, Miss Amy,' said Maria shyly. 'But you should never have risked your life in such a way. Berham told me of the duel.'

'Make sure neither of you ever tells anyone else,' said Amy sharply. 'It was the biggest piece of folly I have ever committed. Are you going to be happy, Maria?'

'Oh, yes, I am marrying a duke.'

'And that is a very difficult thing to do,' pointed out Amy, easing herself up on the sofa. 'Almost like being wed to a member of the royal family. He owns that huge palace down in Cammerside. You will have an army of servants under you and many establishments. You will be a lady of great consequence. Did he say he loved you?'

'Oh, no,' said Maria. 'But he was very practical. He pointed out that he needed an heir and I needed my freedom.'

'That sort of arrangement is all very well for a high-nosed aristocratic lady with nerves of steel.' Amy sighed. 'I fear that unless you stop living in dreams and begin to grow up a little, Maria, you will be crushed by the experience.'

'I must find out where Miss Frederica Sunningdale is residing,' said Maria dreamily. 'Such a charming young lady I met at the inn. I do not have any friends, and it would be pleasant if she could be my bridesmaid. Will Yvette be making my bride gown? Should I wear a veil? I know it is not fashionable to be married in church, but I think I should like that. Do you know a church with really good stained-glass windows? I find it very romantic when different coloured shafts of light strike through a really good stained-glass window.'

'Tcha!' said Miss Amy Tribble.

Miss Spiggs had ingratiated herself so much with Mr and Mrs Kendall on her return from London that she had managed to move into their home as companion to Mrs Kendall. She had also succeeded in worrying them dreadfully about the Tribbles. They did not want to think they had made a mistake, but Miss Spiggs sighed and shook her head and said she feared the Tribbles were adventuresses and not very good *ton*. Amy Tribble was coarse to a fault and Effy was like an ageing courtesan.

So persuasive was she that they were on the point of setting out for London to rescue their daughter when the news of Maria's engagement to the Duke of Berham broke about their ears. As they stared at the day-old newspaper and cried and exclaimed, a letter from the duke was delivered to say he would be arriving shortly.

'So what have you to say to that, Miss

Spiggs?' crowed Mrs Kendall.

Miss Spiggs stood her ground. 'I do not think the Tribbles had anything to do with it,' she protested. 'Maria met the duke at that inn. Remember I told you we was stranded there and he gave a ball.'

'But you said he never even looked at Maria!'

'I didn't want to raise false hopes, but,' said Miss Spiggs, looking modestly down her nose, 'I did put in a leetle word with his grace myself. "You are not married," I said, "and Maria Kendall is the most beautiful girl in the kingdom and has a good dowry." "Miss Spiggs," he said, "you are a wise woman and anyone with a companion such as you must surely be a lady of elegance and refinement."'

'If that is the case,' said Mr Kendall wrathfully, 'I shall ask them Tribbles to give that money back.'

'Oh, they will say I had nothing to do with it,' said Miss Spiggs, 'for they are great liars.' She felt secure. The Kendalls would never be so vulgar as to ask the duke himself how he came to propose.

In this, she underestimated the Kendalls.

A few days later, the duke's footman arrived on the doorstep to say that the duke was staying with a friend in Bath, a Mr Tarry, and begged leave to call.

Mr Kendall promptly sent back an invitation to dinner at five o'clock and then opened his purse-strings wide to impress the duke. Although his house was quite small, he hired ten liveried footmen from an agency. They were to line the steps on either side of the entrance when the duke arrived. His butler, Butterworth, had been a mine manager in the old days, a wiry Yorkshireman with a face like a poacher and blunt manners that suited the Kendalls well, but they had the foresight to warn him to guard his tongue when the duke was present. They also hired a French chef, a Monsieur Duclare, a thin, neurotic creature who specialized in elaborate sauces. Then they felt they should have at least one pretty parlourmaid and appealed to Monsieur Duclare for help, considering that gentleman to belong to the upper echelon of servants. But Monsieur Duclare had been unemployed for some time and had been living on the immoral earnings of one Sally Rutger, a successful prostitute with golden hair, blue eyes, and an easy slatternly manner that made her a prime favourite with the gentlemen of Bath, and so he engaged Sally.

Then, at the last moment, Mr Kendall

rushed out and hired a small orchestra. He then wondered where to put them until his wife suggested they house them in the bedroom over the dining room and get them to play very loudly near the fireplace so that the strains of music would filter down the flue. Just before the duke was due to arrive, the household was crammed to bursting point with servants and musicians. Everyone was quarrelling with everyone else, except Sally, resplendent in tight, low-cut print gown, white gauze apron, jaunty cap with streamers, and red-heeled shoes, who ogled everything in breeches.

The duke felt unusually nervous as he descended from his carriage. He had discounted his mother's remarks about the Kendalls being pushy mushrooms. She was probably thinking of some other couple. She was very muddled and absent-minded these days. The Kendalls were no doubt a worthy, decent couple.

He then recoiled in surprise, for at the sight of him a double line of footmen shouted, 'Huzza! Huzza! Huzza!' and from an open upstairs bedroom window crashed out the strains of 'See the Conquering Hero Comes'.

Feeling dazed, he walked into the hall. The footmen crowded in after him and there was an unseemly scrum as they fought among themselves for the honour of taking his grace's greatcoat.

'Get back, you scum!' roared the butler, Butterworth, and the footmen sulkily filed down the narrow back stairs to the kitchen, where a stream of hysterical French oaths greeted them.

'Sorry about that, your grace,' said the butler, taking greatcoat, hat, gloves and cane. 'Can't get good staff these days.' He ran a calloused thumb over the cloth of the duke's coat. 'Nice bit o' stuff,' he said. 'Bath superfine?'

The duke glared down his nose and said, 'Please announce me.'

'Can't,' said Butterworth laconically. 'Got to pay off that mob,' meaning the footmen. 'Here, Sally, take his grace into the parlour.'

Sally came swaying up to the duke and dropped a low curtsy. He noticed he could see her nipples. She looked up at him roguishly and ran a pink tongue slowly over her lips.

'Is this the home of Mr and Mrs Kendall?' he asked, wondering whether he had arrived by mistake at a brothel that was throwing some sort of a party.

'Oh yes, your grace,' giggled Sally. 'Be so

104

kind as to follow me.'

She threw open the double doors of the parlour and shouted. ''Ere 'e is!'

Mr and Mrs Kendall rose to meet their future son-in-law. Mrs Kendall was wearing so many jewels and necklaces on her massive bosom that she looked like a tray in a jeweller's window. Mr Kendall was squeezed into a pink silk evening coat. His fat face was painted and rouged and the starched points of his shirt were digging into his cheeks. Behind them stood Miss Spiggs, simpering and curtsying.

After the introductions, Butterworth appeared with champagne and Sally carried around the tray of glasses. She handed one to the duke and winked.

'A toast!' said Mr Kendall. 'To the happy couple.'

The toast was duly drunk. 'My boy,' said Mr Kendall, trying to throw an arm about the duke's shoulders, but the duke stepped quickly away, 'you are lucky to be marrying into such a wealthy family, although I am sure you are not short of a bob yourself. Look at my wife's jools. A fortune on that dress alone.' He then proceeded to give the duke an inventory of everything on his wife's person, including where it was bought and how much it cost.

'I am sure our respective lawyers will agree as to the marriage settlements,' said the duke stiffly. He looked away from the Kendalls and his eye fell on Sally, who raised the hem of her skirt to show a well-turned ankle.

'Can't hear that orchestra,' said Mr Kendall. 'What do they think I pay them for?' He bent down and shouted up the chimney, 'Play louder, you monkeys!'

The resultant blast of sound effectively drowned out any further chance of conversation.

They moved through to the dining room. The table was groaning under the weight of gold plate that bore the Earl of Sotheby's coat of arms. Sotheby had lost all his money recently, mused the duke. The Kendalls must have bought his entire dinner service at auction.

As they waited to be served, the orchestra mercifully fell silent, but there came sounds of a fight from belowstairs, French curses, and then the sound of Sally screaming.

'Pay no heed,' said Mr Kendall. 'Servants are the devil. So, your grace, you could have knocked me down with a feather. Mind you, Miss Spiggs here told us she had put a word in your ear.'

The duke looked frostily at Miss Spiggs, who turned as red as fire and then said incoherently that it was just her little bit of fun, just joking.

'Ho, you was, was you?' snapped Mrs Kendall. 'And you saying it was all your doing and blackening the Tribbles' names and saying I had wasted my blunt.'

'Never mind that now,' said Mr Kendall. 'We've got a real Frenchie as a cook, your grace, so you'll get all those foreign messes you society people like.'

The company continued to wait uneasily for their food, all trying gamely to make conversation and all wondering what on earth was happening belowstairs.

The butler entered, followed by Sally. Sally's gown was torn on one shoulder, showing even more delectable flesh, and the butler had a black eye.

He put down a large tureen on the table. From it came the homey smell of beef broth.

'What's this?' screeched Mrs Kendall.

'Not my fault,' said the butler passionately. 'It was them hired footmen got fresh with Sally and that Frenchie starts screaming and hollering and they was all punching and gouging. Then Frenchie runs off after throwing the entire contents of the pots at them footmen. So I went along to the chop-house and ordered the dinner from there.'

'The soup smells excellent,' said the duke. 'Why not serve it?'

This social disaster had the effect of silencing the Kendalls and Miss Spiggs. The duke was able to enjoy his meal in peace. His only worry was how to break the engagement to Maria. For of course he could not marry her. Such in-laws were out of the question. At last the covers were removed, the port was brought in and the ladies retired.

'I must apologize for this evening,' said Mr Kendall. 'I usually keep a good table.'

'On the contrary, dinner was excellent,' said the duke and meant it.

'I need a larger house,' said Mr Kendall gloomily. 'Never thought of it until now.' Then his face brightened. 'Course, we'll be living with you after your marriage, your grace, so the question won't arise.'

'You will not be living with me,' said the duke. 'I am plagued enough with relatives of my own.'

'As you will,' said Mr Kendall, 'but you'll need our advice as to how to handle Maria. Give her a touch of the birch if she annoys you. That's the way she's been brought up.'

The duke thought compassionately of

Maria but then hardened his heart. He had made a rash mistake, a dreadful mistake. He decided to approach the Tribbles and pay them a large fee if they could break the engagement. He did not believe for one moment Maria's promise to give him his freedom should he change his mind.

Maria made her début, without the duke, who had not yet returned, at the Livingstones' ball. She was a great success, as were the Tribbles. Every matchmaking mama wanted to know how they had achieved such a prize for their charge. Frederica Sunningdale was at the ball, and Maria was delighted to renew her acquaintance. They arranged to meet the following day. Beau danced with Maria and begged her forgiveness so humbly that Maria warmed to him. In fact, she felt she could forgive anyone anything, she was so elated and happy at her success. Absence made the heart grow fonder. She forgot about the duke's haughty manner and remembered only that he was handsome and rich.

Maria went out driving with Frederica the following day. Frederica was anxious to hear all the details of the romance, and so Maria obliged, and, by the time she had finished, felt quite sure she really was in love with the duke after all.

Although Amy and Effy were enjoying their success, they still felt uneasy. 'Such a stiff neck as that duke will be shocked by her parents,' said Amy. 'What if he comes roaring back and wants out of it?'

'He cannot get out of it,' said Effy, 'unless he is prepared to face a great deal of scandal and a possible breach-of-promise suit in the courts.'

'I suppose they aren't *that* bad,' said Amy.

Effy sighed. 'Oh yes, they are, sister dear.'

She then noticed Amy had stopped listening to her and was gazing hopefully across the floor. Mr Haddon had arrived.

He walked straight across to them, bowed before Amy and asked her to dance.

Effy bridled as the couple walked away together. It was too bad of Mr Haddon to raise hopes in Amy's silly breast. Also it was not fair of his friend, Mr Randolph, to stay away from so many functions. Her eyes narrowed and she tapped her foot. Amy was not going to steal a march on her. She must not marry. Effy began to plot and plan ways to draw Mr Haddon's attention to herself.

But the duke's return from Bath on the following day soon put any such ideas out of

Effy's head for the time being.

Both sisters knew something was badly wrong when he merely bowed to Maria and said he wished to see the Misses Tribble alone.

Maria left the room, looking worried. While he had been away, she had dreamt of a handsome, lover-like duke, and to see him again as he really was, cold, bad-tempered and withdrawn, made her wish she had never promised to marry him.

'What do you wish to talk to us about, your grace?' asked Effy, after he had been served with wine.

'I met Miss Kendall's parents. Although I did not, after all, ask for their permission to wed Miss Kendall, I fear they gave me their blessing nonetheless. I cannot ally myself with such a family.' He proceeded to describe the dinner party. He was greatly offended when Amy laughed and laughed and finally said she had not heard anything quite so funny in ages.

'But you cannot break off the engagement,' cried Effy, glaring at Amy. 'It would be a great scandal.'

'Exactly. And that is why I am prepared to offer you three times as much as the Kendalls are paying you to persuade Maria that we should not suit.'

There was a long silence while both sisters looked at each other in dismay. Both had been sure the couple would not suit, but they gloried in this great success and that success was worth more than any money the duke could offer.

'We will do our best,' Effy heard Amy say.

When the duke had left, Effy flew at Amy crying, 'How could you promise such a thing. Maria should have been consulted first.'

'Shhh!' snapped Amy. 'Let me think!'

Effy plucked at one of her gauze shawls impatiently while Amy frowned horribly and drank port as if it were water.

'Maria ain't too bad,' said Amy slowly, finally breaking a long silence. 'Head full of dreams. Understandable. But she's a lady. For all their faults, the Kendalls have turned her out a lady. It ain't Maria that needs schooling, it's the Kendalls.'

'Whatever can you mean?'

'I mean, let's see if we can make a go of this. Berham's a cold codface, I'll grant you that, but he ain't nasty or vicious. Make a tolerable husband and Maria can pretty much lead her own life once she's produced a few heirs for him. And after all he's put her through – no, don't ask me. I was told in confidence – I think if she does turn him down, he should be made to hurt a little.

'My plan is this. We get the Kendalls here and tell them flat out they are in danger of spoiling their daughter's chances through their own vulgarity. If they scream with outrage and call off the wedding and drag Maria back to Bath, we'll still get all that money from the duke. If they'll listen to us, we'll get to work on them and turn them out a couple of model society parents.'

Effy shook her head. 'It would not work. It is different with the young. So hard to change the old.'

'Nonsense. I'm going to send off an express today. And I'll make sure they leave that Spiggs woman behind. Great mud-coloured simpering creature with a face like a whipped whore's bum.'

'Listening to the charm of your speech, sister dear,' said Effy sarcastically. 'I am sure you are just the lady to refine the Kendalls.'

They decided not to break the news to Maria of her parents' possible visit to London until they had heard from them.

Lord Alistair Beaumont called that afternoon to ask permission to take Maria for a drive. The sisters gave their consent. Maria had told Amy that Beau had apologized for the scene at the inn, and he was such a handsome man with his long strong legs, curly black hair, and blue eyes that Amy secretly thought Maria would be much better off with him than with the duke.

Maria's heart beat a little faster as she glanced sideways at Beau as he drove expertly through the traffic on the road to Hyde Park. He looked so much like that captain of her dreams.

He asked her if she was going to hear Catalini sing and Maria said ruefully that all her engagements were handled by the Tribbles and so she did not know. 'I should think you will be there,' he said with a smile. 'Rum old birds, the Tribble sisters, from what I've heard. Always guaranteed to turn up at any leading society event. They're a fixture and feature of any Season.'

'I am extremely fond of them,' said Maria quietly. 'Particularly Miss Amy.'

'Ah, your gallant captain.'

Maria blushed. 'So you know?'

'Of course I know. I was Berham's second. What a coil. I don't think anything like that ever happened to Berham in all his well-ordered stuffy life. Sorry. Shouldn't have said that. Fact is, Amy Tribble should have been a man. She'd have been a regular rip.'

'She is really very womanly.' Maria thought compassionately of the glow in Amy's eyes when she looked at Mr Haddon. 'I disagree with you. I think she would have made some man of character an excellent wife.'

'Too old for that now,' said Beau brutally. 'She must be over fifty and most of her contemporaries are dead.'

'She does not seem old to me.' Maria's eyes misted over as she thought of Amy's awkward kindness.

'I declare I've upset you. What can I do to make amends?' Beau reined in his horses and turned to look at her.

The day was fine and warm. Young leaves were budding on the sooty trees in the Park. Maria was wearing a gown of some soft green stuff that showed the excellence of her figure. She was frowning in thought. Then she looked up at him, her green eyes dancing, and he caught his breath. 'I know,' she said. 'Although I do not know whether we are to attend the opera or not, I do know we are going to Mrs Marriot's ball on Saturday. Why do you not ask Miss Amy to waltz with you!'

'And that would please you?'

'So very much.'

'Done! For you I shall waltz with Miss Amy *and* take her into supper. Here comes

115

your beloved.'

Maria looked ahead and a shadow crossed her face. Driving towards them at a smart pace was the Duke of Berham. He had very good eyesight. He saw Beau saying something and pointing in his direction with his whip. He saw Maria look straight at him and saw the worry mixed with trepidation and disappointment on her face. He should have felt glad, for surely such a look meant she was happier with Beau than she possibly could be in his company and that she would be glad to escape from the engagement. But he felt cross and angry.

He reined in his horses and pulled alongside Beau's carriage.

He bowed to Maria and said, 'I am sorry I have been neglecting you, but I have had many matters to attend to.'

'Such as driving yourself in the Park,' said Beau maliciously.

The duke gave him an unfathomable look from his black eyes. 'I shall call on you tomorrow, Miss Kendall.'

'At what time, your grace?' asked Maria nervously.

'At three o'clock.'

Maria's face fell. She had planned to visit the Exeter Exchange in the Strand with

Frederica. She had been looking forward to it immensely. 'I regret I have an engagement at that time,' she said.

The duke thought that the Tribbles had done their work very well and very quickly. 'In that case, I shall see you on Saturday, when I call to escort you to the ball.'

'Very good, your grace,' said Maria meekly.

He bowed and drove off.

'How formal you both are!' exclaimed Beau.

'Are we?'

'Very much so. Do not look so miserable, I pray. Gunter's has just received a new shipment of ice from Greenland. How would you like a strawberry ice?'

'Lord Beaumont, what a splendid idea!'

They drove out of the Park and bowled past the Duke of Berham, who had stopped his carriage to talk to some friends. They were chatting and laughing and did not notice him. But the duke noticed them and felt he had offered too much money to the Tribbles. The task had obviously been an easy one.

The duke said goodbye to his friends and drove to Holles Street. Effy received him with many nervous flutterings. She found the duke quite intimidating and wished Amy had not gone to lie down.

'I congratulate you both,' said the duke. 'I met Miss Kendall in the Park and I could judge from her manner that you had already been successful in persuading her that we should not suit.'

'Oh, no,' said Effy, waving her hands helplessly. 'We have not started yet. Not a word, I assure you. But she is very young for you and she is most certainly not in love with you, so...'

'Did she tell you she was not in love with me?'

'No-o. But you did explain most clearly it was to be a marriage of convenience. I mean, you yourself are clearly not in love with Miss Kendall.'

'Not at all.'

'Then that's all right. Such a relief when no hearts are engaged, don't you think? Tea, your grace?'

'No, I thank you. My mother has returned, I believe, and I must see her.'

The dowager duchess looked up crossly as her son came striding into her boudoir and curtly dismissed her maid.

'And now you are going to give me a jaw-me-dead about that engagement,' said his mother with a sigh.

'And why not?' demanded the duke wrathfully. 'I did agree to let the engagement stand, but that was before I met the girl's parents. Out of the question. What can you have been thinking of to even consider joining our great name with such incredibly vulgar people as the Kendalls?'

'I did not think you were marrying *them*. You need not see them once you are married. The fact is Miss Kendall would suit you very well. Fascinating little creature. She has very pretty ankles.'

'I wish to make one thing perfectly plain to you, Mama. Never again must you interfere in my life, do you hear?'

'Yes, dear. I can hear you, and so can the whole of Cavendish Square. What are you going to do?'

'I have offered the Tribbles money to persuade Miss Kendall not to marry me.'

'You silly boy. She is so very beautiful and so very rich, she can take her pick. She does not need you. The Tribbles would probably have done it for nothing.'

'Am I such an antidote?'

'No, but you are so used to being run after and toadied to that you have quite forgot how to please. You will soon become an opinionated crusty old bore. Now, send my maid back and take yourself off.'

Maria spent a delightful afternoon with her new friend Frederica. They looked at the wild animals in the small zoo, bought trinkets from the booths at Exeter Change, and then strolled down the Strand and across the road and down towards the river.

'We should go back,' said Frederica suddenly.

Maria, who had been discussing books and fashions, looked around her. Tall, ugly, ramshackle tenements reared up on either side. On the entrance steps of one of them, a woman in rags, nursing a baby, held out a claw-like hand for money.

'Let me just give some alms to this poor woman,' said Maria.

'No, no, come away. It is dangerous here,' squeaked Frederica, tugging at her sleeve.

Maria gently disengaged herself and took some silver from her reticule and handed it to the woman.

'She will only spend it on gin,' pointed out Frederica.

'That I won't,' said the woman, for she had heard Frederica, who had spoken quite loudly and clearly, thinking, like most of her class, that beggars were stone-deaf. 'I'll pay my rent and get food for the baby.'

'Who owns such property?' asked Maria wonderingly. 'It is quite disgusting.'

'Duke of Berham,' said the woman, hugging the baby close.

'Come away,' said Frederica, putting an arm around Maria's waist.

'Very well,' said Maria numbly. They hurried back towards the Strand.

'Do not look so troubled.' Frederica peered anxiously at her friend's stricken face. 'Most of these London rookeries are owned by the aristocracy. It's not Berham's fault. He probably does not know such a place exists.'

'Do you think that woman's baby is his?' asked Maria.

'How can you say such things? What put such an idea into your head?'

'I am reading this monstrous fine book called *Jasper's Cruelty or The Wicked Duke*. The duke is quite like Berham, I mean the duke in the novel. And he owns property like this and ruins all the female tenants and then turns them out in the street. Why, Emily – the girl in the book – is most affecting. She stands outside White's Club with her baby in her arms on a snowy night and cries to him as he comes out, "Look upon your son, you dastard"!'

'Maria! I don't think you love Berham one little bit.'

'No,' said Maria. 'I am grateful for that, for I can never marry him now!'

5

Is not marriage an open question, when it is alleged, from the beginning of the world, that such as are in the institution wish to get out, and such as are out wish to get in?

Emerson

Maria sought out Amy, who was lying in her room, nursing her sore, stiff shoulder.

Breathlessly, Maria told her about the buildings off the Strand and then launched into a comparison between the Duke of Berham and the duke in the novel she had been reading.

Amy groaned. 'You are worse than I thought,' she said. 'I have never heard such a piece of silliness in all my born days. Grow up!'

Maria coloured angrily. 'You must admit, Miss Amy, it is disgraceful that he should be the owner of such property.'

'Take it from me, he probably doesn't even know he's got it,' said Amy. 'His agents and men of business handle things like that. Maybe it was not even his agents who bought the wretched place, but his grandfather's. That is not what troubles me. You seem like an intelligent girl to me and yet you can easily dream up a picture of Berham having *droit de seigneur* with a lot of poor women when he could have practically anyone in society he wanted. Young girls' dreams are one thing, Maria; dangerous fantasies are another. If you are looking for a way to break the engagement, then wait and do it gracefully. Don't you want just a little bit of revenge on Berham? He don't really care a fig for you at the moment, and believe me, if you told him right now it was all off, he would probably sigh with relief.'

'Oh, he would, would he?' exclaimed Maria, suddenly furious. 'Then why was he so eager to let the engagement stand?'

'That was before he met your parents. Yes,' went on Amy, surveying Maria's stricken face, 'your parents. Now, Effy and I have invited Mr and Mrs Kendall to London.'

'No!' said Maria. 'Oh, no.'

'Listen. We are going to put it to them that *they* are the ones who need schooling. Think, Maria. If not Berham, then perhaps someone like Beaumont, hey? We'll put a little town bronze on your ma and pa and then you can fly as high as you like.'

'You will find it an impossible task,' said Maria in a low voice.

'I don't think so. I mean, they must be able to recognize ladylike qualities, else how did they manage to make such a good job of you?'

'By beating me?'

'All children are beaten. I must admit they carried it on a bit too long, but that dream-world you live in, Maria, can be infuriating. You must have had some eligible suitors in Bath, or were you determined to not even think of them because they were your parents' choice?'

Maria hung her head.

Amy looked at her sympathetically. 'There, now. Look your best for the ball, and for goodness' sake, stop casting Berham in the role of villain!'

The couple, when they met on the eve of the ball, eyed each other with scarcely concealed dislike. Each was furious with the other for wanting to break the engagement. Each privately thought the other had no right to look so well. The duke was resplendent in black evening dress and a miracle of a cravat. His fair hair gleamed in the candlelight and his strange black eyes had a brooding look. Maria was wearing a pale-pink silk gown decorated with pearl embroidery. Pearls were wound through the thick tresses of her hair and a single row of pearls lay on her bosom.

Effy was wearing a girlish pale-blue muslin gown with a turban made out of swathed blue chiffon. Amy startled them all by appearing in a splendid scarlet velvet gown with long sleeves. It was her evening hat that almost made Effy groan with envy. It was of white satin with a high crown and narrow brim and lined with red satin. The red satin band round the crown was decorated with a crescent-shaped diamond brooch. That brooch sparkled and glittered like Effy's jealous eyes. 'Where did you get that expensive bauble, Amy?' she demanded.

'Mr Haddon sent it to me,' said Amy with a radiant smile. Maria thought with surprise that Amy looked really handsome. The fact was that that glorious present had made Amy feel attractive and fascinating, and when a good-hearted woman feels attractive and fascinating, she quite often is.

'Really,' said Effy crossly, 'I do not know what Mr Haddon is about. It is not at all the thing to send expensive presents to an unmarried lady, and so I shall tell him.'

'Do that,' said Amy with a sweet smile, 'and I shall hang you by your garters.'

The duke looked pointedly at the clock. 'We are already late. It is time to leave.'

'I hear Mr Randolph and Mr Haddon arriving,' said Effy. '*Now* we can go.'

Maria thought it ironic that the two elderly Tribble sisters should be setting out for the evening with their gallants, showing all the pleasure and excitement of young girls going to their first ball, while she simply wished the evening were over. Then she remembered Beau would be there and began to experience some pleasurable anticipation.

The duke began to feel a little sorry for Maria. She was a beautiful girl. Such a pity she should have such terrible parents attached to her like a ball and chain. He would pay her particular attention so that society would think, when the break came, that it was Maria who had left him rather than the other way around.

Maria had been looking forward to dancing with Beau and even hoping he might take her in for supper. She had forgotten she had made him promise to entertain Amy and so she had to be content with the Duke of Berham as a supper partner.

Effy was furious when Beau invited Amy to waltz and then took her in to supper. Really, it was too bad of Yvette to make that hat for Amy and not to dream up a similar creation for her, Effy. Mr Randolph waltzed with her before supper and then both Mr Haddon and Mr Randolph took Effy into the supper room. Normally Effy would have been preening herself at having the company of these two middle-aged beaux, but jealousy of Amy was making her sour and bitter.

Supper was served at long tables in the Marriots' dining room. When Mr Randolph was engaged in talking to the lady on his other side, Effy said to Mr Haddon, 'I am amazed you should send such an expensive gift to poor Amy. It has quite gone to her head.'

Mr Haddon looked across the room at Amy and replied mildly, 'Yes, she is wearing it in her hat. A good idea.'

Effy fanned herself vigorously. 'I only hope you know what you are doing. 'I 'member in ninety-two – or was it ninety-three – when Amy received a diamond bauble from

Colonel Withers and was quite in alt. Of course, his motives were of the worst, and the work I had to do to avert scandal! But at least there was no child.'

'Are you trying to tell me...?'

'My wicked tongue!' cried Effy. 'La, Mr Haddon, it is an old scandal and best forgot. Now do not breathe a word to dear Amy about what I have said.'

Mr Haddon did not reply but pushed his food about his plate with his fork.

'Would you say you are a good landlord?' Maria was asking the duke.

'Yes,' he said. 'My estates are in good order. My tenants have nothing of which to complain. Why do you ask?'

'I was in John Street the other day. You know, one of those narrow streets between the Strand and the river. A shocking place.'

'There are many shocking places in that area. What took you there?'

'I went for a little walk with Miss Sunningdale. What a horrible sight it was. Crumbling stonework, broken windows. That anyone could charge rent from the poor people staying in such a rat hole is beyond me.'

'There is something pointed about the tone of your remarks, Miss Kendall. What has John Street to do with me?'

'You own it.'

'I do? Well, perhaps I do own it. I have a great deal of property.'

'And not a care in the world either,' said Maria. '*You* don't have to live there. I don't think a penny has been spent on the place in years.'

'I leave such matters to my agents.'

'Good landlords, your grace, never leave such matters to their agents.'

'Your parents no doubt being prime landlords, for example.'

'Yes, they are!' said Maria in surprise. 'Papa owns a street of houses in the poorer area of Bath and he makes sure the roofs are always in good repair and that the very poor are not pressed for rent.' She felt a warm glow. She had, she realized, been bitterly ashamed of her parents. It was wonderful to discover virtues in them.

'Then perhaps before tomorrow's church service, you will do me the honour of directing me to this John Street so that I may examine this slum for myself.'

He had hoped to throw her, but she said calmly, 'Gladly.'

He studied her profile in silence for a few moments while he wondered how best to irritate her. 'You have not asked me about my visit to your parents,' he said.

'I hope you were tolerably entertained,' retorted Maria, knowing he was trying to unsettle her and determined not to show it.

'It was a strange meeting,' he said reflectively. 'There were a great many servants.'

'We do not have many servants. The house is too small. They must have been hired.'

'So I gather. I hope for your sake and for your parents' sake that that slut of a parlourmaid was one of the rented ones.'

'Our servants are all respectable. Who is this parlourmaid?'

'A wanton called Sally.'

'Hired.'

Her calm manner was beginning to nettle him. 'Ten footmen of various sizes and different liveries had been engaged to line the steps and cheer on my arrival,' he said. 'An orchestra in some room upstairs played "See the Conquering Hero Comes".'

But Maria had fallen under the influence of Amy Tribble. She put her napkin to her face and snorted with laughter.

She looked up at him with dancing eyes and the duke's normally severe face broke into a charming smile as he looked down at her. The laughter died from Maria's eyes and she felt uncomfortable and short of breath.

'Everyone's behaving strangely,' commented Beau to Miss Amy Tribble. 'There's Berham smiling at Miss Kendall and both seem in high spirits, just when I had begun to think they did not like each other. And now your Mr Haddon keeps looking in this direction and he is becoming angrier by the minute.'

'He might have indigestion,' said Amy anxiously. 'The food is very rich.'

She looked across the room at Mr Haddon, who pointedly turned his head away and then began to talk to Effy with great animation. Effy's blue eyes sparkled and she said something and rapped Mr Haddon playfully with her fan. 'I'll kill her,' muttered Amy through her teeth.

'I beg your pardon?' asked Beau surprised.

'Nothing,' muttered Amy. 'Pass the wine.'

There was one more waltz that evening. Beau managed to get Maria as a partner and Mr Haddon asked Amy to dance.

For a few blissful moments, Amy was happy. All her normal clumsiness fled and she floated round the room in Mr Haddon's arms. 'I am very proud of my brooch,' said Amy.

'Do believe me, Miss Amy,' said Mr

Haddon, 'when I say it was merely a trinket given by one old friend to another.'

A shadow crossed Amy's eyes. 'I did not think it anything else,' she said defensively and then stepped on his toes.

'I was worried that your sad experience with Colonel Withers might have led you to think differently.'

'Who is Colonel Withers?'

'The man who gave you a diamond bauble in ninety-two or around then, and then ... and then...'

'And then *what?*' demanded Amy, stopping still.

Mr Haddon looked this way and that, but Amy's fine eyes were boring into him.

'Why,' he said disastrously, too nonplussed to choose his words, 'Miss Effy said it was a mercy there was no baby.'

'Hear this,' grated Amy. 'I never knew a Colonel Withers, nor would I dream of lying like a trull with any man outside marriage. Effy has been pouring poison in your ears and you think so little of me, so *very* little, that you believed her.' With shaking fingers she unpinned the brooch. 'Take it back. I don't want it now.'

'Miss Amy, I should not have listened to her. Forgive me.'

Amy pressed the brooch into his hand and turned and walked away, leaving him standing in the middle of the floor. Effy was talking to Mr Randolph. She saw Amy bearing down on her like an avenging fury and realized Mr Haddon must have relayed the lies she had told. She squeaked with fear and shoved little Mr Randolph in front of her. Amy picked up the startled Mr Randolph by the arms and lifted him to one side and then seized her sister by the shoulders and shook her till her teeth rattled. Effy began to scream like a banshee. The ladies stood around helplessly and several of the gentlemen were crying. 'A mill! A mill!' and rapidly placing bets on the outcome of the fight. Maria broke through the watching circle and hurled herself on Amy, shouting, 'Behave yourself, Miss Amy. You are a disgrace!'

The sound of her voice made Amy stop hitting and shaking Effy and swing about. She saw the ring of staring faces, the ladies shocked and the men grinning. Effy had slumped to the floor and was crying helplessly. Only Amy knew her sister was as tough as old boots and barely hurt, but Effy looked a fragile and pathetic picture.

She helped Effy to her feet and into a chair. 'Smile and talk, damn you, Effy,' hissed

Amy. 'Look as if nothing has happened.'

Effy rallied amazingly. She raised her fan and waved it languidly. 'The provocation was great, sister dear,' she said. 'But you must not go on so or you will set the fashion for ladies' wrestling.'

Amy burst out laughing, although the effort it cost her to look merry was painful, and the crowd drifted away.

Maria stood before the sisters. 'How are you going to school my poor parents if this is the way you go on?' she demanded.

'I am sorry, Maria,' said Amy. 'So very sorry. But we are famous for our eccentricity. When one is of the best *ton,* outrageous be-haviour is considered eccentric. When one is not, one's social life is ruined.'

Maria was claimed by her next partner and soon found out that what Amy had said was the truth. Everyone seemed to be laughing and joking about the Tribble sisters and saying weren't they monstrous cards and one never knew what they would do next.

She began to look forward to the following morning. The proud and haughty Duke of Berham would no doubt simply stare at his horrible property and turn away. That was the moment when she would tell him the engagement was off.

Amy refused Mr Haddon's escort on the road home, and Mr Randolph, unnerved by her cold behaviour, chattered feverishly to Effy. The duke then told Amy and Effy he would be calling at ten in the morning to take Maria for a drive.

'What an odd time,' commented Amy after they had said good night to the gentlemen.

'I told him about that property of his in John Street,' said Maria, 'and he said he would go there with me and look at it.'

'What is all this?' demanded Effy sharply.

Amy ignored her. She rounded on Maria. 'You surely did not tell him all that rubbish you told me.'

'No,' said Maria. 'I merely told him his property was in disgraceful repair.' She turned to Effy. 'Berham owns some disgraceful rookery in John Street.'

Effy patted her hand. 'All the nobility own disgraceful property somewhere or another. It is most unladylike to comment on it.'

'You are no longer in a position to say what is or is not ladylike,' said Amy.

'I was only joking.' Effy began to cry.

But for once Amy looked on her unmoved. 'I shall never forgive you, Effy,' she said.

She strode from the room. Maria ran after her and followed her up to her bedroom.

'What has happened between you?' she asked. 'Why were you and Miss Effy fighting?'

'The jealous cat told Mr Haddon that I had received a present from a fictitious Colonel Withers who then seduced me, and Mr Haddon believed her! I gave him back his diamond brooch.'

'Miss Effy must have been so very jealous,' said Maria quietly. 'You looked magnificent this evening. And of course Mr Haddon would have been frightfully jealous also – jealous, I mean, of this so-called Colonel Withers. He is a very sensible man and could not have believed such a thing unless he was jealous, now could he?'

Hope and despair warred on Amy's face. 'You see,' went on Maria, 'Miss Effy is very dainty and pretty, quite like a piece of Dresden, and she does try so very hard, and yet it is you, Miss Amy, that the gentlemen appear to prefer. I think you should find it in your heart to be charitable and forgive your sister.'

Amy took off her hat and twisted it this way and that. Then she put it down and ran her large hands through her short cropped hair. 'Oh, I am sure you are romancing again,' she said.

'No, I only weave stupid dreams for myself,' said Maria. 'You'll see. Mr Haddon will send a note tomorrow or flowers or something. And you must forgive him, just as you will forgive Miss Effy.'

'What an odd girl you are,' said Amy. 'Half child, half woman. Do you really mean to break your engagement to Berham?'

'Yes. I shall do it tomorrow. As soon as he sneers at that rookery of his and makes one of his down-putting remarks, I shall tell him.'

'Not much of a revenge,' pointed out Amy. 'He'll probably just be glad to get rid of you.'

Again that strange fury shook Maria. How dare he want to be rid of her!

The morning was grey and overcast with a threat of rain. Great damp gusts of wind sent straw and paper flying about the streets. The duke helped Maria into his curricle. A small tiger was perched on the back, not a boy but a small wizened cockney.

The duke gave all his attention to his horses. Maria was silent, planning a splendid rejection.

They eventually turned off the Strand and bowled down narrow filthy streets until they came to John Street. The duke reined in his horses and his tiger ran to their heads. The duke got down and went around the carriage and helped Maria to alight. He stood in silence, his hands on his hips, his black eyes taking over the buildings on either side.

Then he shrugged. Maria saw that shrug and opened her mouth to begin her breaking-of-the-engagement speech.

But his next words surprised her. 'I suppose it *is* mine. Well, goodness knows I found enough dilapidation on my country estates when I came into my inheritance. It will be more difficult, for there will be all manner of thieves' nests to be rooted out. But I am sure some order can be brought to the place. I shall return with my agent tomorrow.'

Maria could hardly believe her eyes. 'I shall come with you,' she said firmly.

His eyes lit up with mocking humour. 'Meaning you do not believe me. As you will. I think the afternoon would be a more civilized time. You may be shocked at some of the sights if you mean to examine the inside of the buildings with me. Dear God, what poverty! Now, I suggest we make our way back so that we will be in time for church.'

It did not seem the time to make any grand speech. Maria was sure the sights he would see on the morrow would disgust him so much that he would have nothing further to do with it. If he shrank from her parents, what would he make of the wretched inhabitants of John Street? thought Maria, forgetting that the duke was not proposing to have any of them for in-laws.

Mr Haddon and Mr Randolph were both in church. It had become their custom to return to Holles Street with the Tribble sisters after the service. The church was St George's, Hanover Square. Mr Randolph offered his arm to Effy, who smiled at him as she took it. Mr Haddon offered his arm to Amy, who tossed her head and strode off with great mannish steps.

Mr Haddon went after her, caught her by the arm and pulled her round to face him.

'Look at the young lovers,' said the duke to Maria. 'Do you think they know they are in love with each other?'

'You are hardly a judge of who is in love and who is not,' pointed out Maria tartly. 'I do not think you have ever been in love.'

'No, but I am a good observer of the game. Have you ever been in love, Miss Kendall?'

'Oh, yes,' sighed Maria, thinking of all her

dream lovers who always said and did the right thing. 'So many times.'

His face hardened but Maria did not notice, for she had turned her attention back to Amy and Mr Haddon.

'At least let us discuss the matter like two rational beings,' Mr Haddon was saying.

'I don't feel rational. I don't *want* to be rational,' said Amy pettishly.

'Listen to me, Amy Tribble,' said Mr Haddon fiercely. 'I apologize most humbly. You will accept that apology like the lady you are so that we can cease this quarrel and return to our former friendship, which means so much to me.'

Amy blinked tears from her eyes. 'It does?'

'Yes, very much.'

Amy gave him a radiant smile and tucked her arm in his.

'All's well that ends well,' sighed the watching Maria.

The duke looked down at her. 'You must give me the benefit of your experience some day, Miss Kendall.'

'My experience?'

'Yes, you must tell me what it is like to be in love not once, but many times.'

'There will be no opportunity for that, because...' Maria's voice trailed away. She had been about to finish, 'because I am terminating the engagement,' but now was not the time to tell him.

Amy and Effy, to Maria's surprise, insisted on accompanying her and the duke to 'his rookery', as Amy put it. 'For you are in our charge, dear, and you can catch all sorts of nasty infections in a rookery, apart from being raped and robbed, that is.'

The duke was disappointed to have the escort of the Tribbles but did not quite know why.

But his agent, Mr Biddell, most certainly did know why *he* wished the pair in Jericho when they started their tour.

The trouble started in a ground-floor room which housed the woman and the baby Maria had already met. 'As you can see,' said Mr Biddell loudly, 'there is no doing anything with these people. This room is filthy.'

Effy held a handkerchief to her nose and said faintly, 'And so would you be, Biddell, if you had to live here. Broken windows, no food, no money. What is your name, my dear?'

'Betty,' whispered the woman, clutching the baby.

'And where is your husband?'

'Don't have none.'

'Are you a prostitute?' asked Amy abruptly.

'Was,' said Betty. 'Come up to London to get work as a servant and this fellow said as how he would marry me, and once he'd had me, he sort of passed me on.'

'The old story,' sighed Amy. 'Well, something must be done. You can't stay here. That baby needs air and sunshine. How do you get any money at all?'

'I helps the rag-picker.'

The duke was busily writing in a notebook. 'Have you no concern for this poor woman?' asked Maria fiercely.

The duke turned his attention to Betty. 'She will need to be moved,' he said. 'There is a farm labourer on my estate in Sussex who has lost his wife and has two small children. He is an honest, decent man. You look a strong girl, Betty, despite your circumstances. Arrangements will be made to transfer you to the country, where you will look after this man and his children.'

'You cannot send her away like a parcel,' exclaimed Maria.

But Betty had clutched feverishly at the duke's sleeve. 'You mean a man of my own and a house of my own?' she demanded.

'Yes, yes,' said the duke, disengaging himself. 'But see you keep quiet about your past and he will probably marry you. If you philanthropic ladies wish to be of any real help instead of exclaiming at my iniquities, then I suggest you supply this woman and her child with fresh food and clean her up. Now, lead on, Biddell, and stop muttering.'

The sights of the miserable lives in those tenements wrought a change in both the duke and Maria. Maria thought almost fondly of the parents she had so recently disliked and despised. How hard her father had worked to supply her with every luxury, and what a disappointment she had been to him. What were a few beatings compared to the misery these people had to endure? The duke felt his boredom and restlessness and separateness from the rest of the human race slip away as he slowly came to grips with the problem of how to bring some life back into the residents of these horrible, rat-infested quarters. Biddell, who had until that day enjoyed a comfortable, easy life, groaned as the list of the duke's requirements grew and grew. He was to hire armies of scrubbing women, builders, masons, glaziers and carpenters. He did not need to cope with the villains. They had fled as soon as news of the duke's arrival had reached their ears. The worthwhile were to be housed in their vacated rooms until their own were restored and repaired. Any man with any skill living in the tenements was to be employed and paid well. The duke grew so enthusiastic that when a raddled old man of great courage called him a stinking aristocrat living off the backs of the poor, he only murmured vaguely, 'Yes, yes, fellow, but your insults will not help me get anything done. Stop cursing me. Can you read and write?'

'Both,' said the old man. 'Wasn't I a schoolteacher before my lungs gave out and age got me?'

'Well, schoolteacher, here is paper and pencil. Go and make a list of the number of tenants, sex, and clothes needed. Stop glaring at me and do as you are told!'

Maria would never forget that long day. The sky was sullen and a chill wind blew through the cracks in the rickety buildings. The duke's servants, summoned from Cavendish Square, and the agent's men and a squad of workers hired from an agency, ran hither and thither bringing clothes and food. Scrubbing women scrubbed, rat-catchers worked busily from basement to attic, and as soon as one room was scrubbed clean, a family was moved in. The news of the great renovation spread through the streets, along the Strand and up to the West End. Drawn by the news, Beau arrived on foot and found the duke standing in the street, supervising the erection of scaffolding. 'Where is Miss Kendall?' asked Beau.

'In there somewhere,' said the duke in an abstracted tone.

Beau gave him a horrified look and then searched the buildings until he found Maria. She was kneeling down in front of a fireplace in a dingy room filled with pallid children and a consumptive mother, trying to coax a coal fire into life.

'Let me do that, Miss Kendall,' said Beau. 'I was never more horrified in my life. What can Berham be thinking of to let you risk your life in such a place? It must be crawling with infection.'

'It was,' said Maria, straightening up with a sigh, 'but as you can see, even this poor room has been scrubbed clean.'

'They should clean it themselves. You cannot do anything with people like this,' said Beau contemptuously.

'Mind your manners, sir,' said Maria furiously. 'It is hard to keep clean with no water, no food, and no will to live. These people are not deaf, you know.'

'Come outside,' pleaded Beau. 'Berham has armies of people working here.'

'I must find the Misses Tribble first.'

'I should have known they were behind this madness.'

'No, it is I who am behind this madness,' said Maria proudly. 'The duke would not even have known of the existence of this place had I not told him.'

As they went down the stairs, they met Amy Tribble. 'It's the mothers who are the biggest problem,' sighed Amy. 'Like that poor Betty, they come to London as servant girls, get seduced and put on the streets, and so there is no other way they can make a living.'

Maria's eyes gleamed with a crusading fire. 'Berham will know what to do,' she said.

'I say,' came Beau's plaintive voice, 'you aren't going to saddle Berham with the welfare of a parcel of harlots,' but Maria appeared to have gone deaf.

When they reached the street, she ran up to the duke. Beau could see her talking animatedly and noticed the normally stony duke looking down at her with a certain affectionate amusement on his face.

'I think I have a plan for them,' said the duke, 'but you must not expect too much. They are so corrupt, so beaten down, these women, that they would rather I had brought them gin than scrubbing women and clothes for their children. I fear some of them are past saving.'

'But you could *try*.'

'Very well, but do not look so ferocious. You have a smut of soot on your nose. Here, hold still.' He took out his handkerchief, held her chin in his hand and scrubbed her nose. He smiled down at her and then both went very still, Maria wide-eyed and the duke looking at her curiously, the smile dying on his lips. Neither seemed to hear the tremendous noise and bustle in the street.

He suddenly released her chin and said gently, 'You should go home. You have done wonders, but this is really no place for you. Beau,' he called, seeing his friend watching them, 'please escort Miss Kendall home.'

'But you will call on me,' said Maria shyly, 'and tell me what you have planned for these women?'

'I shall call this evening, after dinner.'

Beau collected the Tribbles as well, but Maria found no one to share her reforming enthusiasm on the road home.

'I'm glad that is over,' said Amy roundly. 'Berham is wasting his time. He can organize scrubbing and clothes and fire and food until he's black in the face, but they'll all just wait until he goes away and sink themselves in a stupor of gin as soon as possible.'

'I am sure you are wrong,' cried Maria. 'There must be hope.'

'You live in dreams, child,' said Effy gently.

Maria shook her head fiercely. She felt she had come out into the real world and would never live in dreams again.

'Poverty is a disease, Miss Kendall,' said Beau sententiously. 'You will find they are all responsible for their own condition.'

'I wouldn't go as far as that,' said Amy, remembering her own all-too-recent poverty. 'It's a hard world for women.'

'Not if they accept their role in life,' said Beau with a laugh.

'Which is?' asked Maria.

'To be pretty and winsome and be the support of some fine fellow.'

He was paying attention to his horses and therefore did not see the look of acute disappointment on Maria's face. My last dream gone, thought Maria sadly. What a silly, callous brute!

And yet Beau was not unusual in his views. Like the rest of society, he barely saw the plight of the poor of the London streets. Life was but a journey, and God put each man and woman in their appointed station. Everyone knew a pauper had more chance of reaching the Kingdom of Heaven than a rich man, although all the inscriptions on aristocratic tombs declaring proudly 'He Died Poor' simply meant his lordship (or her ladyship) had rid himself quickly of all worldly goods on his deathbed in the hope that the Almighty would accept last-gasp poverty as a sign of grace.

When they returned to Holles Street, it was to find Frederica Sunningdale waiting for them. She did not appear to find Beau silly in the least. She exclaimed in horror when she learned where they had been and suggested they change their clothes and burn those they had on immediately. Maria grew cross with her, for she longed to find someone to share her enthusiasm. At last Beau offered to drive Frederica back to Lady Bentley, with whom she and her parents were staying, and Frederica dimpled up at him and said shyly she would like that above all things.

'And so Maria handed him over on a plate,' grumbled Amy later as she watched Effy changing.

'What are we to do?' asked Effy.

'I think Maria and Berham were made for

149

each other. They call *us* eccentric! The best we can hope for is to Londonize the Kendalls into suitable in-laws!'

The Tribble sisters, Mr Haddon and Mr Randolph were playing whist that evening when the Duke of Berham arrived. Maria flew to meet the duke, both hands held out in welcome, crying, 'What have you planned?'

He smiled at the whist players and said, 'Pray go on with your game while I talk to Miss Kendall.' Amy and Effy gladly agreed. They had had an exhausting day and did not wish to be bored further with the duke's philanthropy.

The duke had brought a block of drawing paper. He sat down on the sofa in front of the fire and Maria sat next to him. 'This,' he said, sketching rapidly, 'is the outline of a house I own in Gloucester, a country mansion which I seldom use. Now the women and children could be housed there and that radical of a schoolteacher can be put in as overseer. Left to their own devices, I am sure those women would drink themselves to death and so they need to be apprenticed to a trade and earn their living. To that end, I will install weaving machines and they will be taught to make cloth. For the first year, they will be given low wages but will be well housed and well fed. If, by the end of the year, they have proved themselves reformed and responsible, then all the money they get from the sale of the cloth they may keep, or rather, will be kept for them, and a fund will be set up for the children.'

'But some of them are so thin and ill, could they not have a period of rest until they are restored to health?'

'The old schoolteacher, Hart, will see to it that no one is put to work who is unfit. He dislikes me and all I stand for intensely, and yet he will prove to be honest and kind.'

'Do you own more property in London like John Street?'

'I fear so. I can hardly go about moving wagonloads of paupers all over the country, so this is what I plan. Some of the property is on the point of falling down. So' – he ripped off a page and began to sketch again – 'I plan to build a whole village, say, or suburb, on the outskirts of London, with good solid houses and gardens to where the deserving cases can be moved.'

'They could be built around a village green,' said Maria, peering over his arm. 'The children could play there. And you must remember shops. It will be of no use if they have to walk miles and miles to the nearest shops.'

He laughed, put an arm around her and hugged her. 'I see you are out to ruin me,' he said.

Maria blushed furiously and he quickly took his arm away. He looked across at the whist players but their heads were bent over their cards and they had seen nothing.

Maria could almost feel herself being pulled towards his body as though by a magnetic field. Something made her say quickly, 'Is it not delightful? The Misses Tribble have invited my parents to London.'

'Yes, delightful,' he said in a colourless voice. After a few moments, he took his leave. He hoped the Tribbles would get Maria to break the engagement soon. Her parents were unbearable.

Beau seemed very much taken with Maria. Perhaps he would not mind her awful parents. Now the duke came to think of it, Maria seemed to be attracted by Beau. He experienced a sudden stabbing pain over his right eye. It had been a long day. He thought of Maria in Beau's arms. They would make a handsome couple. And he would be free.

Free from what? demanded a nasty little

voice in his head. Harris, the butler, patiently held his greatcoat and the duke stood staring into space. Oh dear, thought the duke. I will not fall in love with Maria Kendall. It just won't do.

Maria went up to speak to Yvette and to play with baby George. For the first time it struck her that the dressmaker was surely in a painful situation. Yvette was quick and intelligent and a genius of a dressmaker. And yet because she was an unmarried mother, she would now be chained to the Tribbles for life and would be expected to be humbly grateful to them.

She told Yvette of the adventures of the day. Yvette was the first to show enthusiasm over the idea of training the women to be weavers. 'It is most important for their dignity that they earn a wage,' she said.

'As you do,' pointed out Maria.

'My wage is a home for my baby and myself, and my food,' said Yvette.

Maria looked at her round-eyed. 'But surely they pay you a wage?'

Yvette gave a Gallic shrug. 'They once paid me a little, but now I think they forget. But I lack nothing. Miss Amy and Miss Effy, when they buy cloth, they tell me, make yourself something as well, Yvette. The best of food from the kitchens comes to me and George. George will have a good education and will be loved. I do not need money. I have nowhere to go.'

'If you did have money,' asked Maria, 'what would you really like to do?'

Yvette had been stitching a lace collar onto one of Effy's gowns. She stopped sewing and let her normally busy hands rest on her lap. 'I should open a little shop in the West End,' she said. 'I should create such fine fashions that royalty would send for me. I should be rich. I would have a fine travelling carriage lined with silk and I would go to Paris and find that wretch who ruined me and I would spit in his face.'

The anger and animation left her face as quickly as it had arisen and she began to sew busily, her smooth head bent over her work.

'My parents are arriving on a visit,' said Maria after an awkward pause.

'That is nice.'

'Well, not exactly. You see, they are very vulgar people and Miss Amy and Miss Effy plan to refine them.'

Yvette looked amused. 'Miss Effy, yes, but Miss Amy's speech is that of a sailor.'

'Only when she is very angry. I do not

think it will work. I think my parents will be furious.'

'And you, mademoiselle, do you think your own parents vulgar?'

Maria blushed. 'Yes,' she said in a small voice. 'I am a great disappointment to them and they are a great disappointment to me. They brought me up to be a fine lady and did not think to refine themselves.'

'I am sure Miss Amy and Miss Effy will think of something,' said Yvette, straightening out a seam. 'They shake people up and then something always happens. But they should be proud of you, your parents, I mean. You are to marry a duke.'

'After he met them, I do not think he wanted to marry me any more,' said Maria.

'Then you are better off without him,' said Yvette firmly. But Maria found that remark very cold comfort indeed.

6

By God! you never saw such a figure in your life as he is (the Prince Regent). Then he speaks and swears so like old Falstaff, that damn me if I was not ashamed to walk into a room with him.

The Duke of Wellington

The arrival of Mr and Mrs Kendall threw the Tribble household into disarray. Trunks and trunks were loaded into the hall and up the stairs. Mr Kendall's butler, Butterworth, resolved not to be done out of a trip to London, had changed himself into his master's valet for the occasion, and, determined not to be intimidated by any grand London servants, stood ordering them about in a way that Effy was sure would soon prompt a revolution in the servants' hall.

The Tribbles had planned to wait a few days until the Kendalls had settled in before dropping their bombshell, but Amy said they would not have a servant left unless she and Effy laid down the law as soon as possible.

But they bided their time until after dinner. Mrs Kendall kept exclaiming that Maria's gowns looked odd and what had happened to all those pretty gowns she had brought to London? Amy, very stiffly on her stiffs, said haughtily that Maria's wardrobe had been too provincial and had had to be altered. This led to an altercation in which both Kendalls told the Tribbles exactly how much each item they had bought for Maria had cost.

When dinner was over, Amy sent Maria to her room and then settled down to brave the Kendalls.

'Mr and Mrs Kendall,' she began, 'what I have to say may distress you, but I want to you to consider my remarks carefully – where are you going, Effy?'

'I am just going to my room to get a clean handkerchief,' said Effy weakly.

'Sit down,' commanded Amy. 'The maid can get it. Now, Mr and Mrs Kendall, after his visit to you, the Duke of Berham decided he could not marry Maria and so he gave signs he wishes to cry off!'

'Why?' demanded both Mr and Mrs Kendall in unison.

'He does not want you for in-laws,' said Amy bluntly. 'He thinks you are too vulgar.'

'And after all the money we spent on him!'

raged Mr Kendall. 'That jackanapes is not getting out of this engagement or I'll have him dragged before every judge in the land. He shall not break my child's heart.'

'Your child is not in love with him. In fact, she was so sure he would regret the engagement after he had seen you that she promised to let him off the hook should that be the case. So far, he has obviously not reminded her of her promise. Instead, he has offered to pay us a handsome sum should we be able to help him get free.'

'I don't believe a word of this,' said Mrs Kendall. 'Lor! The lies Maria do tell.'

'In this case, she is not lying. We invited you to London because we feel somehow that Maria and Berham are in their way well matched. It is not Maria who needs schooling,' said Amy roundly while Effy moaned faintly in the background, 'it is you yourselves.'

'How dare you, you frazzled old hen,' cried Mr Kendall. 'I could buy and sell you.'

'You cannot buy or sell the manners of a gentleman,' said Amy, losing her temper. 'If I am a frazzled old hen, then you, sir, are a fat, grunting porker, sweating in your stays, and stinking abominably of musk and unwashed arse.'

Mr Kendall rose to his feet and then went and helped his fat wife out of her chair. Holding Mrs Kendall's hand, he turned to face the sisters.

'We shall leave in the morning,' he said, 'and we shall take Maria with us, and you two will return every penny I've paid you or I will sue you, so help me.'

There was a long silence after they had left. Then, 'How could you, Amy?' demanded Effy. 'Such vulgarity on your part, and such cruelty. You should have used finesse, delicacy.'

'A fat lot of good you were,' said Amy. 'You left me to do the dirty work. Never mind, Berham will pay up. We shan't lose.'

'We will lose our successful reputation,' said Effy tearfully. 'I do not believe for a minute that Maria promised to release the duke. She made that up.'

'I don't think she did. She hadn't that dreamy look in her eye when she told me. Look, Effy, it was all doomed to disaster anyway. Maria don't want Berham and he don't want her.'

'But she won't want to go home either,' said Effy quietly. 'She is probably crying her eyes out.'

But upstairs, Maria was still elated after her

first successful battle ever with her parents. They had come to tell her to pack and leave. They had tried to berate her but with less than their usual force, for Yvette's creation of a gown lent Maria dignity and poise. So Maria with flashing eyes told them she had never wanted the duke but that when she returned to Bath, things were going to be different in the Kendall household.

It was only long after they had gone that Maria began to feel very low. The duke would hear of her leaving and of the end of the engagement from the Tribbles. She would never see him again. She would never have a chance to watch the building of that model village. She began to retreat back into dreams. These were not her real parents. Her real parents were a foreign prince and princess who had smuggled her out of their country for fear she would be assassinated. She would be parading in the Pump Room in Bath among the querulous invalids when a group of exotically dressed warriors would burst in headed by the man she had been betrothed to in her cradle, Duke Ivan. He would ride his horse straight into the Pump Room and bend down and lift her up beside him and they would ride off, scattering in-valids to right and left. 'And a very thoughtless and cruel thing that would be, too,' said the voice of Maria's conscience, but the hurting side of Maria who lived on dreams shouted back, 'Shut up,' and went on to embroider the dream that might keep reality at bay for a little longer.

It was a gloomy morning for Amy Tribble. She rose early. She heard Maria moving about her room and went to talk to her, but Maria had a dreamy look in her eyes and barely seemed to hear her. 'My wretched tongue,' thought Amy miserably. Her back ached and she could feel one of those dreadful waves of heat beginning to engulf her body. She wanted to hug Maria and beg her forgiveness, but whatever dream encased Maria kept Amy at bay.

She trailed back to her own room. Her eye fell on a prayer stool in the corner, seldom used. What could God do to help one silly ageing virgin? But surely, thought Amy, there was no harm in asking. Perhaps God answered all prayers but often the answer was no, which made people like herself think He had more important things to do. Praying that Maria might marry her duke after all was surely worldly vanity. But then, Maria's happiness was not. Amy sank to her knees and bowed her head. She would pray for Maria's happiness and forgiveness for her own folly and then just wait and hope.

The Kendalls were ready to leave by three in the afternoon. Their round little figures were still stiff with outrage as they came down the stairs, holding hands.

Harris, the Tribbles' butler, held open the door. Amy and Effy dropped low curtsies. Then, as they all stood in silence, Maria came down the stairs, and Amy winced when she saw her reddened eyes. Obviously, Maria's dreams had not been strong enough to keep grief away forever.

And then Harris looked out into the street where the footmen were strapping the Kendalls' boxes and trunks onto the roof of their enormous travelling carriage when his jaw dropped. He turned and said in a croaking voice, 'It's His Royal Highness, ladies, and he is coming here.'

'Slap me,' said Mr Kendall faintly.

The Prince Regent had heard about the Tribbles' fight at the ball and had laughed very much, and so that had led to more anecdotes about the Tribbles being poured into the royal ears. The prince had met the two sisters briefly in the past but he was now determined to call on these eccentric wonders.

He entered the hall and looked about him in great good humour. Effy and Amy sank into court curtsies, as did Maria. Mrs Kendall tried to copy them and ended up sitting down on the floor. Mr Kendall bowed lower and lower until he over toppled and stretched his length at the royal feet.

The prince roared with laughter. Stories about the Tribbles had recently become the fashion at elegant dinner tables, and he was delighted to think he would be able to come out with some really new adventures.

'Please step this way, Your Royal Highness,' said Amy. To the prince's glee, Amy and Effy stepped over the fallen Mr Kendall as if he did not exist and led the way upstairs.

In the drawing room, seated in front of a cheerful fire and with a glass of the very best burgundy in his fat hand, the prince looked around him with pleasure. He was not interested in Maria; it had been a long time since young women had taken his fancy. For a long time now he had preferred women older than himself. The Kendalls had crept in and were standing, looking at him in awe.

Their dumbfounded admiration pleased this normally unpopular prince. 'Who are these people?' he asked.

163

The Kendalls moved closer together for comfort. Surely Amy Tribble was going to tell the Prince Regent of their vulgarity.

'Miss Kendall is our latest charge,' said Amy. 'She is engaged to the Duke of Berham. Allow me to introduce her parents, Mr and Mrs Kendall of Bath. They are staying with us before the wedding to acquire some town bronze.'

'Most important, hey,' said the prince expansively. 'Sit down by me, Kendall.'

Trembling, Mr Kendall released his wife's hand and moved across the room gingerly as if walking on broken glass. He sat down in a chair next to the prince, his fat body shaking like a jelly.

'So you run a sort of school for manners, Miss Effy?' said the prince, casting an appreciative eye over Effy's dainty figure and cloud of silver hair.

'Yes, sire,' said Effy. 'We have been most successful.'

'So I hear. None of our aristocracy will be safe from you. Damn me, if learning manners and bowing and scraping ain't a harder thing to do than fight a war.' The fat royal face clouded over. The prince had begged to lead his troops into battle and had not been allowed to go.

164

Mr Kendall found his voice. 'But, sire, with your royal presence always before us in the country to set an example in manners and dress and decorum, it can only do good, bring a refining example into the coarsest bosom.'

'You're a fine fellow, Kendall,' said the prince expansively. 'I like your style but not your coat. Put yourself in these ladies' hands and they'll soon have you looking as fine as fivepence, hey?' He turned his attention back to Effy. 'But you are not leaving us? I saw a monstrous carriage outside with all sorts of bags.'

Effy looked wildly to Amy for help and Amy said smoothly, 'Mr and Mrs Kendall are just arrived.'

'Welcome to London,' said the prince.

Mrs Kendall began to cry and he looked at her like a pouting baby. 'What's the matter with that woman?'

Mrs Kendall sank to her knees. 'Oh, sire,' she sobbed. 'I am overcome with the honour. I shall treasure this moment until the day I die.'

The fat royal face cleared and the prince looked vastly pleased. He would talk about this at dinner. 'Woman was so overcome by our presence, she fell on the floor and burst into tears,' he would say.

He rose to his feet. 'We wish you well, Miss Amy, Miss Effy. Make sure you do not refine Mr and Mrs Kendall too much. There is an honest simplicity in their manners which pleases us.' He bowed to the company, squeezed Effy round the waist, patted Maria's hand and wished her well in her forthcoming marriage, and took his leave.

Amy took a deep breath. 'Harris,' she said, 'Mr and Mrs Kendall will be staying after all. Take the bags off the coach again.'

Effy waited nervously for the Kendalls to refuse. But they were still shaken and awe-struck. Amy looked at Maria. But Maria's eyes were still clouded with dreams and she did not seem to have heard.

Amy was to say afterwards that it was the first time the house in Holles Street had really been turned into a school. The carpets were rolled up in the drawing room, and every afternoon Effy would sit at the piano while Maria danced with her father and Mr Haddon danced with Mrs Kendall and Amy sat in front of them like a ballet master, rapping out the time with a long cane. 'And *one* and *two* and … no, no, *no,* Mr Kendall,' Amy would cry. 'You bow with a flourish.

Do show him, Mr Haddon.'

Maria was enjoying the change in her role with her parents. Now it was she who was passing on all her knowledge and training that she had learned from dancing masters and deportment mistresses and governesses. But deep inside her was a niggling sorrow that neither the duke nor Beau had called. Amy had not told her that all callers other than Mr Randolph or Mr Haddon had been refused admittance.

When the dancing was over, Mr Kendall received further instruction in important matters such as how to open a snuff-box with one hand, how to carry a quizzing-glass, how to hold a muff, how to make calls, how *not* to mention the price of everything, and how to remain silent on all subjects he knew nothing about. Mrs Kendall had to work on her curtsy, put most of her jewellery back in the jewel box, and learn the novelty of changing her linen at least once a week instead of once every three months. Amy found to her distress that she was beginning to like the Kendalls immensely and the fact that they trusted her to see that Maria did marry the duke after all felt like a heavy burden on her shoulders. She was so intent on schooling them that she did not have much time for Yvette and baby George.

Yvette was beginning to feel ill-used for the first time. Usually after she had remodelled the wardrobe of whatever charge the sisters had taken on, she could manage to take things easier. But now she had Mrs Kendall's gowns to cope with and designing and stitching for a very large woman meant hours of sewing.

She would have found her life very hard indeed had not Mr and Mrs Kendall begun to find her little sewing room a refuge from the terrors of fashionable schooling. They were sorry for Yvette and adored her baby. Mr Kendall bought George a splendid baby carriage made of cane and lined with blue silk and he and Mrs Kendall delighted in taking the baby to the Park. In her way, it was Yvette who did more to encourage them to go on with their schooling than Amy or Effy. She would sit and stitch and say in her practical way that society was hard and one had to know the rules and play the game. It was of no use pointing out that Amy Tribble had a coarse tongue, for everyone knew the Tribbles were good *ton* and once you had become accepted, then nothing you could do could make you unacceptable unless of course you were a virgin who erred or a wife who paraded her affairs.

Slowly the schooling began to take effect. Although the Kendalls might still be coarse inside, they had quickly learned to remain silent. Mrs Kendall began to present a fashionable appearance, and when Mr Kendall's new clothes arrived from the tailor, Amy decided it was time to break their seclusion.

Amy went out on calls around her friends looking for a suitable occasion to launch her new charges, an occasion where the duke would be present.

At last she arranged with Mrs Marriot that a *fête champêtre* in the Surrey fields would be just the thing, provided the recent good weather held. Amy decided to take a gamble and gave Mrs Marriot money towards the expense, enlisting that lady's help in seeing that the Kendalls did not disgrace themselves.

Maria was more nervous than her parents when the day of the fête arrived. For the first time in her life, she was on easy terms with them. 'Don't know how you put up with all this, Maria,' her father would groan after an exhausting afternoon in which Mr Randolph, who had been press-ganged into helping, had given him instruction of how to raise his hat, how to wear it at exactly the right angle, and how to carry a bicorne, that collapsible hat, under his arm when wearing full dress.

The day dawned sunny and pleasant, a rare occurrence at the freakish English weather sseemed to delight in breaking on the very day some society hostess had planned an outdoor event.

They made their way to the Surrey side in open carriages. Mrs Kendall was glad she was allowed to wear one of the new Leghorn straw hats, for the Tribbles had forbidden her to carry a parasol until she learned the proper use of it. This quite bewildered Mrs Kendall, who had previously thought one used it simply to keep the sun off one's face, but it now appeared it could be a deadly social weapon, lowered or dipped at just the right angle to depress the attentions of the pretentious or twirled occasionally to show off the silk covering. She was told to remember her fan must always be carried by the *end,* which had to be pinched between the fingers, and on no account to open it until such time as the sisters were able to teach her the intricate language of the fan.

'Cannot I just use it to keep cool?' Mrs Kendall had protested, but it seemed the fan was one of those originally useful things, like a quizzing-glass or walking-stick, that had acquired a whole list of dos and don'ts.

Maria was wearing a white muslin morning gown with a blue sprig and a pelisse of pale-blue sarsenet. Her wide-brimmed straw hat was lined with blue satin, and blue satin streamers fell from the crown and down her back. She kept wondering if the duke would be there and wondering nervously what he would think of her parents, yet she was determined to snub him should he show them any coldness. Mr and Mrs Kendall had been instructed to keep out of the duke's way, should he put in an appearance, as much as possible. They were doing very nicely, Amy had said, but they had a long road to travel.

To Maria, they were still the old parents and she could not see much change in them apart from their new easy manner towards herself. But Mr Haddon, who was travelling with them, thought there was a marked change. Mrs Kendall in wine-coloured silk looked a plump and dignified figure, and Mr Kendall in a well-fitting coat, pantaloons and Hessian boots looked like a gentleman for the first time.

Maria's dream lovers had come between her and the duke and she had almost forgotten what he looked like. When she set eyes on him as they alighted from the carriages she was startled to find he was so very handsome. For his part, the duke felt a lifting of his spirits when he saw Maria. At first he did not recognize the couple with her as the Kendalls of Bath, and when he did, he began to wonder if he had been too hard on them. They were so quiet, so sedate, and so impeccably dressed that he could not quite believe they were the same people.

He asked Maria to walk with him for a little. Maria glanced up at his profile and made up her mind. The engagement had to be broken. There was no point in playing silly games and waiting for him to show some softer feeling. He never would. She doubted if he would ever be capable of romantic feelings towards any woman.

'I am glad of this opportunity to speak to you,' said Maria.

'You would have had plenty of opportunities to speak to me had you granted me audience,' he said. 'I became quite weary of being told that you were not at home.'

'No one told me you had called.'

He looked down at her in surprise and was all at once furious with the Tribbles until he reminded himself that he had offered them money to turn Maria against him.

'What is it you wish to say?' he asked curiously.

'If you will remember, I promised you that if you took my parents in dislike, then I would release you from the engagement.'

'Yes, I do remember.'

'Then you are free, sir Perhaps your secretary would be so good as to send an announcement to the newspapers to the effect that the engagement has been ended.'

It was what he had wanted … was it not?

And yet he had so much to tell her. He had wanted to show her the architect's plans for that village. He had wanted her to drive out with him and inspect the site. No one else was interested. His agent was sulky and his mother thought he was mad. His friends said that coddling the poor would start a revolution, and it was courting disaster not to keep them in their proper places.

'I did not say I disliked your parents,' he said stiffly.

'But you implied you found your visit ridiculous.'

'As you did when I told you of it.' She looked cool and pretty. A warm breeze was blowing across the field. An errant tendril of hair blew across her cheek.

Maria dug the point of her parasol into the grass and twisted it. 'So shall we say it is at an end?' she said.

'Walk a little with me.' The duke took her arm. He felt hurt. It was what he was sure he had wanted, and yet he felt hurt. 'Perhaps we should leave it a little. Your parents must be enjoying their visit. Would it not be kind to leave our announcement until later?'

'How much later?'

They had walked over a rise and the rest of the guests were hidden from view. 'Just for a little,' he said. 'Besides, I wanted to show you the site I have chosen for my model village.' He gave an awkward laugh. 'My friends tell me I have run mad and I dearly need someone to share my enthusiasm.'

'Very well.' Oh, why did she sound so reluctant, thought the duke crossly. 'Where is it?'

'South of Bethnal Green. Beyond Jews Walk, there is Bonners Hall, and beyond that, open land which I have purchased.'

'I would like to see it,' said Maria.

'Perhaps I could take you there tomorrow?'

'You must ask my parents' permission.'

'I shall do that.'

They walked on in silence.

174

'Who are these lovers of yours?' he asked abruptly.

Maria coloured angrily. 'I have no lovers, sir.'

'You told me you had been in love many times.'

'Oh!' Maria looked up at him shyly. 'Dream lovers, that is all. Every young girl has romantic dreams.'

What a splendid day it was, thought the duke. He had really never before noticed what a jolly place the English countryside was. He thought quickly. If Maria's parents knew he was going to take her out driving as far as Bethnal Green, then they might say they would come, too, or they might insist she took her maid.

'I do not want to be on bad terms with your parents,' he said. 'They might be like my friends and disapprove of my plans. I shall simply tell them I am taking you for a little drive without saying where.'

'I think they would approve of your plans,' said Maria, 'but, if you wish, I shall let them think we are going to the Park. We have walked a long way from the other guests. Do you not think we should turn back?'

He obediently turned around. Maria was very conscious of the pressure of his arm.

She kept remembering that kiss at the inn. Some imp prompted her to say, 'I wonder who I shall marry. Can you recommend anyone?'

'With your face and fortune, you may have your pick,' he said sourly.

'A merchant or some man of the professional class?'

He did not reply. He seemed to retreat into himself. Maria longed to make him smile at her again. 'How is Betty?' she asked.

'Betty?'

'The woman with the baby in John Street.'

A flash of amusement lit the duke's eyes. 'Betty was taken to the country by my reluctant agent. She has settled in very well but affects grand London airs and says loudly she is not accustomed to the company of peasants.'

'I am sure that cannot be true,' said Maria. 'Your agent does not like the extra work and therefore is telling you tall stories.'

'I believe him. He does not like hard work, I agree, but I know him to be honest.'

Maria walked on in silence, her face averted. 'What did you expect?' he teased. 'A humble and grateful Betty? Roses round the door and love in a cottage? Endless gratitude?'

That was just what Maria did expect. 'The poor are not always worthy,' he went on. 'How can they be? Their minds and bodies have been warped for so long.'

'Then why take the trouble?' demanded Maria.

He looked surprised. 'It is my duty. A duty I am grateful to you for bringing to my notice.'

'A duty? Did no pity move you? No warmer feelings?'

'I cannot indulge in pity or warmer feelings, or the sights of London would break my heart. Come, Miss Kendall, what would you have? Were my emotions involved, then I should spend my life being bitterly disappointed when my charitable efforts were met with sullen ingratitude. I am realistic.'

'And not romantic?'

'I do not waste my time in idle fancies.'

But as they approached the guests and Beau strolled up towards them, his blue eyes dancing with pleasure at the sight of Maria, the duke mentally picked up Beau, carried him by the seat of the trousers across the field and dumped him face-down in a cow pat.

He moved off to talk to the other guests and did not notice that Frederica Sunningdale had joined Beau and Maria and that Beau seemed more interested in Frederica than in Miss Kendall.

The duke approached the Kendalls and bowed. Mrs Kendall dropped a correct curtsy and Mr Kendall gave a stately bow in return.

The duke said the weather was fine and the Kendalls murmured their agreement. He said Maria was looking very attractive and both smiled and nodded. Intrigued by this change in the normally garrulous Kendalls, he was about to see if he could extract some speech from them when Amy Tribble appeared on one side of him and Mr Haddon on the other. Amy pointed with her parasol away from the Kendalls and said the champagne was about to be served. The duke turned and looked as well, and when he turned back, the Kendalls had disappeared into the crowd.

'I was going to ask the Kendalls' permission to take Miss Maria driving tomorrow,' he said to Amy.

'You may have my permission,' replied Amy, 'although I think you should leave the girl alone. This is not the way to encourage her to break the engagement.'

'It is one way to give her social consequence

which will stand her in good stead once the engagement is over,' he pointed out.

'A very true if smug remark,' said the irrepressible Amy.

He wanted to join Maria again but she was surrounded by a group of courtiers. One was holding her parasol over her head, a second was holding her fan, and a third was offering a glass of champagne to her. He stood and watched her. She did not once look in his direction. He turned away and began to flirt easily with several of the young misses who were present so that his entourage might rival Maria's, but every time he looked across at her, she was laughing at something someone had said and appeared to have forgotten he was at the party.

She would not be allowed to behave so once they were married, he thought. Then he remembered they were not to be married, that he had offered the Tribbles money to see that they should never be married, and that Maria herself was eager to break the engagement. At this, he thought the party a cursed flat affair, damned the Season as a load of silly frippery and heartily wished the whole business were over and done with.

7

Leisured society is full of people who spend a great part of their lives in flirtation and conceal nothing but the humiliating secret that they have never gone any further.

George Bernard Shaw

'Now, sister,' said Amy sternly, 'when Berham comes to call, do *not* look pleased to see him.'

'But, why?' wailed Effy. 'There was a point yesterday when I thought they would suit very well. Surely only Maria would take an interest in those charitable schemes of his. Any lady of the *ton* would consider it a waste of money.'

'We did not consider it a waste of money when we were so very poor and Mr Haddon gave us coal.'

'That was a present,' said Effy huffily. 'No lady accepts charity.'

'Which is why so many of them starve and leave a household of fat servants behind when they die,' said Amy roundly. 'If Berham thinks we're all eager to see him marry Maria, then he will turn cool. The Kendalls will be out with baby George when he calls – I have seen to that. They did very nicely yesterday.'

'So sweet the way they dote on that baby.'

'George is a darling.' Amy suffered a pang of conscience. Yvette had so much work to do – too much. She eased her conscience by promising herself to see to it that once Mrs Kendall's gowns were completed, Yvette should have several weeks free.

'If you say so, I shall be cool to Berham,' said Effy, standing on tiptoe to look in the mirror and adjust one of her many gauze shawls about her neck. 'But I have been thinking, Amy. If Maria does not wish to marry him, then we stand to gain a great deal of money from Berham and we could take a little rest. We could perhaps have next Season all to ourselves.'

'Won't do,' said Amy. 'London eats money. And we must start putting something by for our old age. Mind you, we already *are* old.'

'You may be, sister, but I am in my prime.'

'We are twins – or had you forgot.'

'Age is all in the mind.'

'Fiddle,' said Amy crossly. 'Age at this moment has settled in the small of my back and it aches like the devil.'

Effy tweaked a curl and eyed her sister speculatively. She herself was suffering from back pains, strange heat, and swollen ankles. She was frightened to send for the physician, for he would bleed her and leave her feeling weak. Perhaps she should discuss her symptoms with Amy. But Amy had that wretched diamond brooch back again, pinned on the front of her gown, and jealousy decided Effy against confessing any weakness to her sister.

While Effy and Amy prepared for the duke's call, Mr and Mrs Kendall put George in his new perambulator and headed for the Park. 'You know,' said Mr Kendall, 'I'm blessed if there ain't a prime piece of business under our noses.'

'Whatever do you mean?' Mrs Kendall looked fondly down at George, who was clutching a toy soldier firmly in one chubby hand.

'That Yvette. See here, how many ladies complimented you on your gown yesterday? Lots. Did any of those grand folk in Bath ever say a word about your dress? Never. When I think what a mint one pays dressmakers in Bath. Imagine what a really good one could earn in London.'

George gleefully threw his soldier in the

direction of a dowager and Mrs Kendall clucked fondly as she retrieved it, trying for the dowager's sake to pretend she was angry with George and not succeeding very well. 'Do you mean you are going into the dressmaking business, Mr Kendall?' she asked.

'Not me. Yvette. I could buy her a shop. All grand and tasteful, like. She sets up in business and I take a percentage of her earnings once she's got on her feet. She'll need to have seamstresses and a nurse for George. Take a lot of money, but I'll swear it will pay back well.'

'Them Tribbles would be furious,' pointed out Mrs Kendall. 'Remember, they're friends of the Prince Regent.'

'They'd come about,' said Mr Kendall easily. 'Now, that Amy, she looks the strong one, but she's got a heart like butter. They could've turned Yvette out into the street, baby and all.'

Mrs Kendall looked doubtful. 'Miss Amy and Miss Effy won't like the idea of having to pay through the nose to get gowns made for them.'

While Yvette's future was being discussed, the Duke of Berham was seeing Miss Amy Tribble at her grandest. She was a stately figure in dove-grey silk, made with a high

183

neck edged with a small ruff of lace, Yvette having at last persuaded her that low-necked gowns were unflattering. She wore a grey gauze turban and heels to her shoes, which gave her extra height, making her almost as tall as the duke.

'We just want to assure you,' said Effy, who had been well schooled by Amy, 'that we will do everything in our power to persuade Maria to end the engagement.'

'I do not wish you to turn her against me,' said the duke sharply. 'Leave the girl to make up her own mind.'

'It is for her own good,' said Amy. 'You would not suit, and it is not as if it is a love match.'

'Miss Kendall tried to terminate the engagement yesterday,' said the duke abruptly. 'I told her it would be kinder to let matters rest while her parents are in London. I beg you, say no more on this matter to Miss Kendall at present.'

'As you wish,' replied Amy, with seeming reluctance.

By the time Maria appeared, the duke was anxious to take his leave. He told the Tribbles they would be out for some time, as Maria wished to see a little more of London.

Maria noticed as she approached the

carriage that his tiger was not present. She also noticed that his hand rested lightly on her waist for a moment as he helped her in.

The fine weather had broken, and although there was no rain, it was chilly with an irritating, frisky wind, blowing straw about the street and snapping in the blinds and awnings over the shops and houses. Because of the recent sunshine, all London had hoisted full sail. Every house and shop in the West End had its buff or striped canvas awning so that the sunshine should not fade either the goods in the shop windows or the carpets in my lady's drawing room.

Maria was wearing a Polish robe of purple velvet ornamented with gold cord and tassels at the waist and edged with fox fur. On her head, she wore a jaunty Polish cap with a peak and cord and tassels hanging from the right side of the crown. On her hands were York tan gloves, and on her feet, gold kid half-boots.

The duke was aware of every inch of her. Because the Tribbles had made her appear forbidden fruit, he was sharply conscious for the first time how very seductive her body was, how thick and glossy her hair, and how perfect her skin.

That kiss at the inn did not count, he

found himself thinking. What would it be like to kiss a willing Maria, a pliant Maria?

The carriage bowled swiftly along. Maria clung on to the side and enjoyed the novelty of speed. Soon they were through the village of Bethnal Green, past the grim walls of the workhouse and out into open fields.

He stopped his team and pointed across the fields with his whip. 'Here,' he said. 'What shall I call it? Maria's Town?'

Maria laughed. 'I think we should let the new residents decide on a name.'

He leaned under the seat and brought out a large sketchbook and began to outline the plans for the new village. 'It would be a semi-rural community,' he said. 'There would be shops and a village green and a duck pond.'

'And a church,' said Maria eagerly, 'There must be a church. And can it be one like a real church and not one of those things that look like ballrooms?'

He quickly sketched a church with a steeple. He was very good at it, thought Maria, watching a picture of church and shops and houses growing up on the page.

She was leaning against his shoulder as he sketched and he was intensely aware of the warmth of her body and the delicate flower perfume she wore.

He wanted all at once to throw down the sketchpad and take her in his arms, but for the first time in his life, he was afraid of a rebuff. Men of his age and rank usually had a great deal of experience of women, but the duke had had surprisingly little. He had lost his virginity at the hands of an experienced courtesan at an early age – for that was one of the things one did, like learning fencing and boxing – and the experience had killed a great deal of the romanticism in his soul. His following affairs had been brief and matter-of-fact, the termination of each settled by his lawyers. His few past mistresses would have been amazed had they guessed that one day the chilly Duke of Berham would be sketching plans for the welfare of paupers, longing to take a young lady in his arms, and afraid of doing so.

They talked for a long time, Maria's enthusiasm for his plans increasing her attraction for him.

'We should go back,' he said reluctantly, 'but perhaps we have time to make a slight detour on the road home. I found I own some more property in bad repair, just outside the City, in St Charles Street. The builders have already moved in and the poor wretches have been given clothing and food.

Would you like to see it?'

'Oh, yes,' said Maria. 'These poor people must be so grateful to you.'

'No, I should not think so,' he said calmly, but as they drove back, Maria wove rosy dreams of grateful men and women clustered round the duke, kissing his hand and calling him a saint.

Maria's dreams began to fade as they turned down among mean, sinister streets. She was acutely aware of the richness of her gown, of the splendour of the duke's bearing, and of the red eyes that glared up at them as they passed.

The duke stopped his carriage at the end of St Charles Street, and then sighed. Maria looked down the street in horror. Men and women were tearing down the wooden scaffolding that had been erected by the builders and were throwing it on a bonfire. On one pavement, other men and women were handing over bundles of new clothes to a man with a cart and receiving money in return. On another corner, a gin shop was doing a roaring trade.

And then one of the wretches saw him and pointed. There was a cry of 'There he is!' But no one came forward to kiss the duke's hand or thank him. Instead, a woman bent down and picked up a cobblestone and threw it straight at the carriage. The duke caught it and dropped it to the ground. Then he seized the reins and swung his team about and drove off as fast as he could just as a rain of missiles struck the back of the carriage.

After he had gone some way and the mean streets fell behind, he glanced down and saw that Maria was crying. He drove into the courtyard of a coaching inn in the City, tossed the reins to an ostler, and then helped Maria down, putting an arm around her shoulders and leading her into the inn. People looked up curiously as they entered the coffee room and he guided her into a booth in a far corner where they were screened from view and called for a bottle of wine. He sat down next to Maria and took out his handkerchief and gently dried her eyes.

'Come now,' he said softly. 'There is no reason to be so upset. You are making me feel guilty. I am a brute to have taken you there. I should have guessed what might happen.'

'S-so ungrateful,' sobbed Maria, all her rosy dreams in ruins.

'It was too much, too soon,' he said. 'Proper charity is hard work, not just handing out clothes and food and walking away. What should I do? Call in the constable and the militia? I must return tomorrow when they are quiet and subdued again and get to work trying to rescue those that might be saved from those that are too sunk in depravity. Here is our wine. Drink up and you will feel better. You cannot expect high ideals, honesty and courtesy in a rookery. These people are further down than the people of John Street. All they have known is poverty, thieving and gin to alleviate the misery. Hope and respectability are frightening and threatening to them, and charity is an insult.'

Maria shuddered. A piece of the rookeries seemed to have entered her soul. She could smell the filth and still see the barefoot children in their dirty rags with the urine streaks down their legs, the red-eyed gin-sodden women, the orange-cheeked babies, the scabs, the bent legs, the wizened bodies. She could still feel the hate.

'If you are hell-bent on turning reformer,' he went on, 'then you must harden your heart and be prepared for a lifetime of disappointment. You must believe that if only a few are turned to a decent life, then all your efforts are worthwhile. Never expect gratitude for giving away what you can easily afford. You must be prepared to work with these dreadful people or forget they exist and return to the West End where we are sheltered from such a world.'

'I do not think I can ever forget them,' said Maria.

'What a shameful pair we are,' he laughed. 'Society would be horrified.'

Maria sipped her wine and leaned against him, still too overcome to worry about the fact that his arm was around her shoulders.

They fell silent. The coffee room was dark and smoky and low-raftered, and they were isolated in their corner from the rest of the customers. He raised her hand to his lips. Maria shivered and said weakly, 'We should return. They will be wondering where we are.'

He tilted her chin up and smiled down into her green eyes. His mouth approached hers. 'No,' whispered Maria.

He frowned slightly and released her chin. Then he muttered something impatiently, gathered her in his arms and brought his mouth down on hers. At first Maria dimly told herself it would be vulgar to struggle or make a scene in a public inn. Then her emotions swept up and engulfed her. The kiss went on for a very long time. The waiter popped his head over the settle and asked, 'Will there be anything else, sir?' and shrugged and walked away as 'sir' remained deaf and blind to everything but the girl in his arms.

The duke felt weak with passion, roaring, blinding red passion that surged in his ears like the sea, making him forget place and time.

To release her was like a bereavement. He looked at her, stunned and dizzy. And then from somewhere in the room, the clock struck seven.

'The deuce,' he whispered. 'We must go. They will wonder what has happened to us.'

It was unfortunate for the duke and Maria that the frantic Tribbles had gone to his town house in search of their missing charge, leaving the equally frantic Kendalls to pace the floor.

When the duke arrived back in Holles Street with Maria, he was met by an enraged Mr Kendall, demanding furiously to know where they had been.

The Kendalls listened in horror as their glowing daughter told them of her afternoon.

'You risked our girl's life, taking her to the worst parts of London,' shouted Mr Kendall,

all social training forgotten. 'Do you know what we've spent on that girl to bring her up a lady?' He furiously spelled out prices of governesses, dancing masters, Italian teachers, music teachers, ending up with the vast sum he was paying the Tribbles.

'Control yourself, sir,' said the duke, looking down his nose. 'Your daughter was safe with me.'

Mr Kendall turned an odd sort of puce. 'Who are you, sir? I say, who are you, sir, to take that hoity-toity tone with me? Well, we don't need you or your title and my Maria shall not marry you. So there. Take yourself off and never come near her again.'

'Gladly,' said the Duke of Berham. He turned on his heel and left, just as the Tribbles arrived home.

'The engagement is off,' said the duke furiously. 'Kendall has broken it himself. I must consider myself fortunate to have escaped from such a family.'

'It was what you wanted,' said Amy faintly.

He climbed into his carriage and drove off without answering while the Tribbles went indoors to cope with a distraught Maria and a raging father.

The duke drove home, went into his library, called for brandy and slumped down in a chair in front of the fire. A terrible coldness began to come over him and he began to feel quite ill.

For it dawned on him at last that he wanted Maria Kendall, horrible parents and all, and he would do anything in the world to get her!

Amy sat in Maria's room and held her hand. 'There, there,' said Amy, 'the man is a brute and quite, quite about in his upper chambers. Does he take you to the ring in the Park? Does he suggest a visit to the opera? No. "Come and see my filthy, dirty places," says he. Tcha! Romance is dead.'

'I wanted to go,' said Maria fiercely. 'This is a man I could love, or so I thought. And then because Papa berates him, he stalks off with never a thought for anything but his own dreadful pride.'

'Take comfort from that,' said Amy. 'He would make a nasty husband. Have your parents spoken to you?'

Maria sighed. 'At great length. They have changed in that they no longer want to hit me. They were kind and actually apologized to me and said that ambition had turned them into monsters. But it is not really I or you who have changed them, but George.'

'George?'

'Yes, Yvette's baby. They dote on him. George can be naughty at times, but they laugh indulgently and hug him. I was never allowed to be naughty.'

'If George were their own, they'd probably whip his arse,' said Amy cynically. 'He's not theirs, but Yvette's, and so they can go on being sort of doting grandparents. We shall come about, Maria. Plenty of men at the Season.'

But Amy felt very low as she trailed off to Effy's room. Effy was weeping quietly.

'I need support,' said Amy, plumping herself down on the end of Effy's lace-covered bed. 'What's to do?'

'We are ruined,' said Effy. 'The announcement about the termination of the engagement will be in all the newspapers tomorrow. Berham will not pay us anything because it was Mr Kendall who ended the engagement, and Mr Kendall said that the money he spent on us was wasted and we would not get any more, and although he paid generously in advance, he was due to pay more at the end of the Season. What are we to do?'

'Advertise again,' said Amy with a cheerfulness she did not feel. 'People would have come running to us if Maria had married

Berham. In fact, they might have come running already if that wretched couple had not gone out of their way to demonstrate to society how little they care for each other. Damn Berham! May syphilis eat off his nose!'

'Amy!'

'May the gout plague him, may the whores rob him, and may his charity cases stone him and burn him, the stiff-necked fool. He was in love with the girl and she with him, I swear. What other couple of fools in Christendom would want to interfere in the lives of trulls and thieves?' said Amy with all the forthright callousness of the eighteenth century, which did not bend to this sickening sensibility of the early nineteenth.

'Oh, what are we to do?' wailed Effy.

'We'll ask Mr Haddon and Mr Randolph.'

'Oh, yes,' agreed Effy, grateful. 'Gentlemen always know what to do.'

Mr Haddon and Mr Randolph gravely listened to the problem the next morning as they shared breakfast with the sisters.

Mr Randolph thought Mr Kendall had behaved just as he ought. Berham had behaved shockingly. No one knew of that kiss. Their shock was reserved for the duke's philanthropic efforts. Not that he should make them, but that a man who commanded so many people should stoop to get involved himself.

'Maria will retreat into dreams again,' said Mr Kendall.

'She's suffering but she's given up dreaming,' said Amy. 'Bless me, but I think that dreadful St Charles Street woke the sleeping beauty at last. I don't know whether she misses him or his charity cases. Fact is, Mr Haddon, we wondered if you would take another advertisement and put it in *The Morning Post* for us. We must forget Maria and look to our future.'

'Gladly,' said Mr Haddon, 'but I fear the case of Maria and Berham is hopeless and you can consider yourself well out of it.'

Which all went to show that men were not much use at all, said Amy Tribble after they had left.

She was sunk in gloom. Why could not Mr Haddon have offered to marry her? Did it never cross his mind?

Her thoughts were interrupted by Mr Kendall. He had talked long into the night with his wife. They felt they were doing their duty in breaking the engagement, but they decided they owed a debt to the Tribbles.

Both were enjoying their new social ease and anxious for more lessons from these friends of the Prince Regent. And so the amazed Amy found Mr Kendall was offering her more money to continue schooling him and Mrs Kendall.

She was so elated by this news that when the Duke of Berham called, she felt able to face him.

Effy was summoned. Effy did not yet know the latest piece of good news and was still tearful.

'I will come to the point straight away,' said the duke, looking anywhere but at the sisters. 'I offered you a handsome sum to release me from that engagement.'

'And you are going to tell us that you ain't going to pay because Kendall broke it, not us,' said Amy.

'I am come to tell you I will pay you anything you wish if you will see to it that the engagement stands.'

Effy looked at Amy and Amy looked at Effy.

'What can we do?' cried Amy.

He smiled at her and Amy realized with a start that he was devastatingly attractive. Her eyes dropped to his well-muscled legs. Yes, definitely attractive.

'I am sure you will think of something,' he said. 'I believe you always do.'

After he had left, Amy ordered champagne. Once again her nerves seemed to be stretched to the breaking point and she did not feel quite sane. She hoped the champagne would cool her.

She and Effy drank and discussed and dismissed various ways of getting the duke and Maria together.

'Pity, that's it!' said Amy suddenly.

'Whash a piddy?' slurred Effy.

'Maria. She's got a lot of compassion and all that. She must be made to feel sorry for him. Let me see.' Amy glanced at the clock. 'He's no doubt down in St Charles Street. I shall go there and tell him my idea.'

'Come too,' said Effy, blinking like an owl.

'No, you'd better go to sleep. You're foxed.'

Amy hurtled downstairs and ordered the carriage. She took two footmen with her for protection.

The sight that met her eyes in the middle of St Charles Street made her glad she had decided to bring a bodyguard along. A circle of men and women were surrounding the duke and a great brute of a man. Amy strode up and demanded, 'What's happening?'

'A mill,' said a dirty woman. 'Our Bert's going to draw 'is grace's cork.'

The duke had not found a docile population when he had returned to St Charles Street. It was almost as if they had been waiting for him. Almost as if they had had this bruiser, Bert, drafted in from somewhere to confront him. It was, however, not unusual for one of the lower orders to challenge an aristocrat to a fight. The social laws did not interfere when it came to every Englishman's right to bloody the nose of another. Often, like Bert, they made the mistake of thinking all aristocrats effete. But men like the duke, thrashed at home, thrashed at public school, trained from an early age to endure pain, sent to the wars, and then trained in delicate social arts like boxing, were tough and fit. If an aristocrat survived his upbringing, he was usually very strong indeed. Only those who had the luck to come into their inheritance when they were still in short coats could lead a life of carefree indolence.

So he had removed his coat and prepared to do battle. Amy's brain worked quickly. If the duke was injured, then she could tell Maria, and Maria's kind heart would be touched and she would come and sob at his bedside. But just to make sure the duke was not actually killed, Amy gently eased a pistol she had had the foresight to prime and bring along out of her reticule. She saw a gin bottle on the ground and picked that up as well. Then she noticed a pamphlet lying at her feet, and under the feet of the mob she could see many other pamphlets. Still holding the pistol, she tucked the gin bottle under her arm and picked up the pamphlet. 'Citizens, rise against your oppressors,' screamed the black type. 'Come to the Methodist Hall tonight and hear Dr Frank preach on the equality of Man.'

'Seditious bastard, whoever he is,' muttered Amy. There was a cheer as the fight began.

To the crowd's disappointment, it did not last very long. The duke danced lightly around his opponent and then struck like lightning. It was a massive blow, and Bert crashed onto the cobblestones while the duke stood over him nursing his bleeding knuckles.

A reluctant cheer went up and the crowd parted to let him through.

He walked blindly past Amy, his coat, which he had picked up off the ground, slung over his shoulder.

'Oh, God, for what I am about to do, please forgive me,' said Miss Amy Tribble, and she lifted the gin bottle and gave the duke a sharp and efficient crack on the back of the head. He reeled and staggered. 'Catch him and put him in the carriage,' shouted Amy.

As the duke was hoisted in, Amy saw his agent and servants clustered at the end of the street. 'You cowards,' she shouted.

'Why did you hit 'im on the head, missus?' demanded a woman, clutching at Amy. Amy shook her off. She had to get the duke away before any more onlookers began to spread the word that she had deliberately struck the duke, who was now unconscious.

The duke was laid out on the seat of her carriage by the two footmen. Amy climbed in and pulled down the window and called up to the coachman, 'Drive on, fool. What are you waiting for?'

As the coach began to move, Amy heard a loud voice shouting. 'Don't let the rich scum escape. Hang them. Burn them.'

Amy stared in the direction of that voice. A ginger-haired man in showy clothes had climbed up a lamp-post to address the crowd.

Amy knew that face. It was Frank, the ex-second footman, who had caused rebellion in her servants' hall and then had fled. He saw her and ducked down the lamp-post and disappeared into the crowd.

But Amy quickly forgot about Frank. The duke lay very still, his face white.

'What have I done?' whispered Amy. 'Perhaps I have killed him.'

She raised the trap and ordered the coachman to drive to the duke's town house in Cavendish Square.

The Dowager Duchess of Berham came slowly down the stairs as her unconscious son was carried into the hall. She leaned heavily on her stick and asked in a flat voice, 'Is he dead?'

'No,' said Amy, 'but get a physician. I think he is only stunned,' while inside she prayed to God and all his angels to spare her from the gallows.

She turned to leave as the duke was slowly carried up the stairs.

'No! Stay!' cried the dowager. 'I must know what happened.'

She commanded the housekeeper to put Amy in the Yellow Saloon. Amy waited in an agony of fear. They would probably hang not only her but Effy as well, assuming Effy to be a conspirator. Her mind see-sawed wildly.

After an hour of pure hell, the door opened and the dowager came in. 'He is recovered,' she said.

Amy put her head down and wept with relief.

The dowager sat beside her on the sofa and put a comforting hand on her shoulder. 'There, there. All is well. You have had a bad fright. He is very strong. He will need to rest, however. His wits seem to be wandering. He is talking about being in some fight and that as he was leaving, you struck him down from behind. Before he lost consciousness, he heard someone asking you why you had struck him.'

Amy flinched. She had been so sure that the duke had been totally unaware of her presence.

'I did strike him,' she said in a low voice. 'I meant it for the best.'

'Meaning you thought the world would be better off without him?'

'Oh, no. You see he is in love with Maria Kendall, but her father has forbidden the marriage and I thought if he were ill or injured, Maria might rush to his bedside and … and…' Overwrought, Amy began to cry again.

'You are a very bad woman,' said the

204

dowager in a matter-of-fact voice. 'But I shall forgive you if your plan works.' She rang the bell and then walked over to a writing-desk in the corner and began to write. When a footman entered, she ordered him to take the note to Miss Kendall, and to make sure it was delivered to her personally.

When the footman had gone, the dowager went back to sit beside Amy. 'Now, Miss Tribble,' she said sternly, 'dry your eyes and let us get down to business. The Kendalls are common, but I believe them to be rich.'

'Oh, yes, very rich,' said Amy weakly. She took out a large handkerchief and blew her nose.

'You are sure of this? Might they not be showy and vulgar people who put on a display of wealth but are constantly in debt?'

'No, I happen to know that Mr Kendall pays cash for everything. No debts. I found out that much when we were in Bath.'

'You advertise for difficult girls, do you not? What is the difficulty with Miss Kendall?'

'Dreams, that is all,' said Amy. 'She used to live in a dream-world. Her parents bullied her too much, you see. But she is gentle and kind and most young girls have heads filled with nonsense.'

'And some old ones,' pointed out the dowager maliciously. 'You take your duties seriously, Miss Tribble. Do you usually risk gentlemen's lives in order to bring your charge to the altar?'

'Please ... I must apologize ... not myself.'

'We will see how it works. If it does not work, then you will be damned by me and society as a dangerous and silly old woman; if it does work, and I hope it does, for I have a feeling in my bones that Miss Kendall will do very well for my son, then you will have my lifelong support for your ventures. Please stop crying. Tears do not become you; nor do they make me feel sorry for you. It will be a great coup for you if this comes off. Believe me, the Kendalls should consider themselves fortunate that such as we should stoop so low. Why did the silly man break off the engagement?'

Amy told her of the duke's drive with Maria.

'Ah, well, I see his point. My late husband left all the squalid side of things to his agent, and quite right too. The only time we ever concerned ourselves overmuch with the welfare of underlings was when it seemed we might have an uprising like the Terror in France. Some of my friends even apprenticed their children to a trade. Trade! Can you imagine it?'

'Easily,' said Amy, recovering some of her spirit. 'I am in trade myself, as are all women who push their sons and daughters into marriage.'

'We take marriage very seriously,' said the dowager, 'and quite right too. You would not mate a fine racing horse with a coal horse, now would you, and expect the outcome to be worth anything? I hear someone arriving. Let us hope it is Miss Kendall.'

The butler entered carrying a card on a silver tray, which he presented to the dowager. 'Miss Kendall,' he said.

Amy let out a slow breath of relief. 'Do not relax so soon, Miss Tribble,' said the dowager sharply. 'You are not out of the woods yet.' She turned to the butler. 'Take Miss Kendall directly to his grace's bedchamber, usher her in, shut the door behind her and tell the other servants not to go near.'

'What did you say in your letter?' asked Amy curiously.

'Why simply that my son was at death's door and that she should come and say her last goodbyes.'

Amy's face broke into a grin. 'And they call *me* ruthless,' she said.

8

Unarm, Eros, the long day's task is done,
And we must sleep.

Shakespeare

Young girls do not mature and give up dreaming overnight. As Maria hurried to Cavendish Square, she was in the grip of a fantasy so morbid it was like a nightmare.

He would die before she got there. He would never know she loved him. His death-rattle sounded in her ears. Perhaps he really loved her after all, and her father's breaking of the engagement had made him take his life.

On receiving the dowager duchess's note, she had fled the house without telling her parents and had hired a hack.

When it stopped before the great house in Cavendish Square, she could hardly bear to look at it in case the hatchment was over the door and the mute already wailing on the steps. But one furtive glance told her she still had hope. That was until she stepped down and paid off the carriage and noticed that straw had been laid on the street outside the house to muffle the sound of the traffic.

The butler who opened the door to her looked so grave and so funereal that she felt quite faint. She waited in an agony of hope and despair until he returned and, with a bow, said in deep mournful tones, 'Follow me, miss.'

How slowly he mounted the stairs! Was it because the duke was already dead and there was no longer any need for haste? She longed to ask the butler, and yet fear of hearing the worst kept her silent.

The butler went on up to the second floor and along a shadowy corridor lined with all the paintings the Berhams considered too inferior for public view. Rain had started to fall outside and the wind soughed around the building like a banshee.

The butler held open a door and bowed low. Maria slowly entered the room and he closed the door behind her.

The duke was lying on the bed, his eyes closed. His head was bound with bandages and his face was very white.

Maria ran and flung herself on the bed crying, 'Don't die. Please don't die.'

The duke's eyes flew open. He had been

given a sleeping powder by the doctor and was feeling groggy. He thought vaguely it must be some sort of dream. Maria Kendall was lying on his bed. But with all the single-minded opportunism of the true aristocrat, he decided to make the most of the dream while it lasted.

He dreamily unfastened the ribbons of her bonnet and threw it on the floor and unpinned her hair so that it cascaded about her shoulders.

'You are alive,' whispered Maria.

'Oh, it's not a dream,' he said. 'You really are here.'

'Your mother told me you were gravely ill.'

She was lying beside him, her head on the pillow next to his own.

He raised his head up, twisted round, leaned on one elbow and looked down at her.

'Marry me,' he said. It was a command, not a question. 'Yes,' said Maria. 'But wh–?'

Her question was silenced as his lips came down on hers. Sweet gentle kisses soon lost their innocence, to be replaced by hot, searching, probing kisses, inflamed by the exploration of his roving hands along her body.

Passion and modesty warred in Maria's breast and passion won.

At last, his hands stilled. He raised his mouth from hers and smiled down at her tenderly. 'How soon can we be married?'

'I do not know,' said Maria, dazed with love and kisses. 'What if my father will still not allow it?'

'We'll elope,' he said dreamily. 'We'll run away together, far way from those interfering harridans.'

'I cannot allow you to speak thus of my parents!'

'Not your parents, you goose; Amy Tribble and my mother. Why do you think I am in bed with my head bandaged? Amy Tribble followed me to St Charles Street and hit me on the head, brought me back here unconscious; and now I learn my own mother is in on the plot and sends you a letter saying, in effect, that I am dying.'

'Amy Tribble hit you on the head? Why?'

'Because, my sweeting, I promised the Tribbles money to make sure the engagement was not broken and this is Miss Amy's way of going about it.'

'How very terrible,' said Maria. Then she began to giggle. 'How v-very terrible.'

The duke began to laugh as well. Then he said, 'Since her plot *has* worked and here I am and here you are, we may as well enjoy ourselves before the inevitable interruption.'

'Has he got her clothes off yet?' demanded the dowager duchess.

Amy Tribble straightened up from the keyhole of the duke's bedroom door, her face flaming.

'No,' she said gruffly. 'They're lying *on* the bed, kissing.'

'Leave them a bit,' said the duke's mother. 'May as well be sure.'

'Anyone in my charge,' whispered Amy fiercely, 'stays a virgin until her wedding night.'

'I didn't,' said the dowager crossly. 'Waste of time.'

Amy bent down and applied her eye to the keyhole again. The duke's hand slid down Maria's body and then began to slide up under the skirt of her gown.

'Damme! That's enough!' roared Amy, opening the door.

Maria struggled up, blushing. The duke lay back with his hands behind his head, hands that had quickly been removed from the more interesting parts of Maria's body the minute he had heard Amy's shocked outburst outside the door.

'I hope, your grace,' said Amy, 'that you

will wait for the wedding.'

'And I hope, Miss Tribble,' he said coldly, 'that you will realize how lucky you are not to be charged with assault.'

'That wasn't me. It was another woman,' lied Amy. 'Come along, Maria. It is time for you to return to your parents and tell them the good news.'

But to Maria's horror, Amy's fury, and Effy's distress, Mr and Mrs Kendall refused to give their permission. Mr Kendall had 'been treated like dirt' by Berham, he said. He had been thinking over what Amy had told him. For Berham to wish to be released from the engagement because he thought them, the Kendalls, too vulgar, was the outside of enough. It was time Berham had his comeuppance.

In vain did Maria plead and Amy rage. Mr Kendall was adamant.

Mr Haddon had moved to a tall thin house in Chapel Street, which he now shared with his friend, Mr Randolph. Mr Randolph was at his club and Mr Haddon was alone when a distraught and tearful Amy arrived on his doorstep.

'You cannot enter,' he said after his butler had startled him with the news of Amy's arrival. 'Think of your reputation, Miss Amy!'

'A pox on my reputation,' shouted Amy, beside herself with worry. 'I wish I *had* a reputation to lose. I'm too bloody old and ugly to have a reputation. Oh, damn it all to hell. I wish I were dead. I wish them poxy Kendalls were face-down in a cesspool. I'm sick of respectability. I'll keep a brothel, that's what I'll do. Better money and less worry.'

Curious heads began to pop out of windows of houses across the street.

Mr Haddon drew Amy inside and shut the door. 'I do not think entering my house can damage your reputation more than you have just damaged it,' he said severely.

He led the way into the front parlour and sent his curious butler off to find the port decanter.

'Now, try for some calm,' he said, 'and tell me all about it.'

And Amy did, in fits and starts, ending with, 'Do you see what this means? Berham was going to pay us for fixing the marriage; Kendall was going to pay us handsomely for schooling. Now, neither will pay us, and all society will know we have had our first failure. Why, Mr Haddon, you are laughing!'

'Miss Amy, you do not realize what you have done! You talk about hitting Berham on the head with a gin bottle as if it were the most everyday happening.'

'It may sound like that now,' said Amy miserably. 'But I near died with fright and worry at the time. Tell me what to do!'

Mr Haddon poured port for them both and settled back in his chair. 'I think we should see Berham and persuade him to elope with Maria.'

'Elope? But what of our reputation as models of propriety?'

Mr Haddon bit his lips to stop himself from smiling. 'What you must do,' he said, 'is present Mr Kendall with a bill for your services to date. Then you must get Berham to agree to the elopement and exact his promised fee from him before he goes. Surely that will give you enough to take a rest before thinking about taking on anyone else. Miss Effy is looking quite worn down with worry, and she is not as strong as you.'

All in that moment, Amy could have hit *him* with a gin bottle.

'Effy has nerves of steel,' she said coldly. 'She is a better actress than I, that is all.'

'We will go now and see Berham,' said Mr Haddon firmly. 'Oh, I know it is near midnight, but I think he will be glad to have this matter resolved. Then you may tell Maria of the arrangements and ask her to look in good spirits. You will get your money out of Kendall easier if he thinks you have been instrumental in making Maria forget Berham. When the Kendalls learn of the elopement, pretend to be shocked and swear you know nothing of it. Once they have returned to Bath, we shall put it about society of how you arranged all. Society will consider you matchmakers extraordinary. They will think it incredible that anyone managed to get the proud Duke of Berham to elope.'

Despite the late hour, the duke received them in his bedchamber. As he listened in amazement to the news of the Kendalls' continued refusal of his suit and to the plans for his flight to Gretna, he wondered what ever had happened to his stately well-ordered life. Then he calculated, after Amy had fallen silent, that it might work out very well after all. He would be spared the horrors of a society wedding and he would be able to have Maria all to himself as soon as possible.

'Very well,' he said. 'But strange as it may seem, Miss Amy, I am quite capable of arranging my own elopement. All you have to do is tell Maria to wait for word from me. Now I am anxious to get some sleep. It is not every day I am hit on the head.'

Amy looked mutely towards Mr Haddon for help. He cleared his throat. 'Your grace, you kindly promised the Misses Tribble a generous fee for arranging the happy outcome of your engagement. As you will be pressed for time in the days to come and may forget...'

The duke grinned. 'If you had not damaged my wits, Miss Amy, I would not pay you one penny and I would send you the physician's bill as well. Bring my portable writing-desk over to the bed.'

Amy twisted her gloves in her hands as he wrote a draft. He handed it over. She took out her quizzing-glass and studied it. It was a magnificent amount. She made up her mind. They would have the whole year to themselves. No work. No difficult girls. No frights. No worries. Nothing but peace and calm. She would pluck up courage to consult a doctor about her aches and pains and soaring temperatures.

'Thank you,' she said quietly. 'Thank you very much.'

Maria was roused at one-thirty in the morning by Amy shaking her awake.

Her eyes were red with crying. Gently

Amy whispered the plans for the elopement.

'But my parents. They will cast me off,' protested Maria.

'No, they won't,' said Amy, crossing her fingers behind her back. 'I'll see to that. Don't worry about a thing and leave everything to me.'

'You are so good to me. I am sorry to disappoint you. It would be wonderful if you could have paraded a grand wedding before society.'

'No need for that now,' said Amy. 'You can always get married in church when you come back.'

'If you are sure my parents will not be furious…?'

'No, no. All they need is to be presented with the *fait accompli* and they'll be merry as grigs. Just you sit tight and wait for word from Berham.'

Effy cried with relief when Amy told her about the elopement and the money. 'The only thing is,' said Amy, 'I do hope the Kendalls are not too sore about it, for I have taken a certain liking to them.'

But the events of the next few days were enough to turn Amy and Effy against the Kendalls. Mr Kendall certainly paid his bill and said he was grateful to them for their schooling and amazed that they had managed to cheer Maria up so quickly. But then Mrs Kendall led Yvette into the room and the trouble started.

'We have news for you, ladies,' said Mrs Kendall with a motherly beam. 'You will be losing Yvette.'

'You cannot go with them,' cried Effy aghast. 'You cannot hide yourself in Bath and waste your skill on...' Her voice fortunately trailed off, for she had been about to say something very rude indeed.

'She ain't going to Bath,' crowed Mr Kendall. 'I'm setting her up in her own business in the West End. Got a neat little property. Rooms above the shop, a nurse for baby George and near enough the Park to get fresh air.'

'And what have you to say to this, ma'm'selle?' demanded Amy wrathfully.

'I am so grateful,' said Yvette simply. 'I will be my own mistress. I will give you special rates.'

'Ho! You will, will you?' said Amy. 'Is this how you repay us?'

'Stow it!' said Mr Kendall brutally. 'You wasn't even paying her a wage, and if we hadn't taken George out to the Park, the mite wouldn't have seen a peep of daylight this age.'

The fact that all this was true and made Amy feel bitterly guilty only added fuel to her wrath. Now Yvette's marvellous creations would be available to anyone who could pay and not reserved for them alone. She raged, she pleaded, and she cajoled, but Yvette would not be moved.

Luckily for Yvette, a note arrived later that day with plans for the duke for the elopement, and so the sisters' attention was momentarily diverted and she was able to take her leave with surprisingly little fuss, although both sisters did break down in tears at the last moment as baby George waved a chubby fist in farewell.

They turned their full attention on Maria. She was to leave in two days' time at dawn. The duke's carriage would be waiting outside. There was a bustle of packing and planning, all to be done in secrecy.

The great morning arrived. The sisters, in wrappers, nightgowns and fantastic nightcaps, stood on the step of their house on Holles Street, waving goodbye. Maria hugged them fiercely, begging them to send her love to Frederica Sunningdale and her apologies to her for not being able to engage her services as maid of honour.

The carriage turned the corner of the street and disappeared.

'Another one bolted,' said Amy sadly, 'and left us the mess in the stables to clean up.'

'I am glad it was not a wedding in London after all,' said Effy. 'You know, it always serves to remind me that we are still … are still…'

'I know.' Amy put an arm about her sister's shoulders. 'Come inside. The morning is chilly.'

Maria had left a note for her parents in which she said the Tribbles knew nothing of her elopement, but that did not stop most of Mr Kendall's wrath descending on the Tribbles' heads. He ranted and raged and told them they were a disgrace until Amy, exasperated, ordered both of them from the house. Mr Kendall demanded his money back, and then Effy and Mrs Kendall had to stop him from striking Amy after she had told him in which part of his anatomy she would like to lodge his money.

To Effy's relief, the angry couple took their leave without any further demands for repayment. They left the Tribble sisters feeling shaken and sick.

Amy and Effy, strangely enough, would have been even more furious if they could have heard a conversation between the couple on the road to Bath. For after berating the Tribble sisters and cursing them and leaving them both feeling as if they had been in the wars, the Kendalls were slowly waking up to the fact that their daughter had made a very successful marriage indeed.

'You know, my love,' said Mrs Kendall, putting a hand on her husband's knee. 'I am wondering why we are in such a taking. Our daughter is to be married to a duke.'

Mr Kendall snorted furiously. Then he began to think about it. He was going back to Bath, where despite all his money and all his efforts, he had been cruelly snubbed so many times. He was about to become father-in-law to a duke. He looked down at his new clothes. The Tribbles had done their stuff, right enough. Why, his wife looked even better-gowned than some of the titled ladies in the Pump Room. He began to dream. He would be questioned about the elopement. He would say casually, 'That young jacka-napes of a duke was down on his knees begging me for Maria's hand but I did not think him at all suitable. A bit too old, hey,

Mrs Kendall? But the silly things must need run off to Gretna. Still, they will be married in London on their return. You want to come to the wedding, my lady? I'll see, I'll see. So many people to invite, don't you know.' And so Mr Kendall dreamt, while far to the north on the road to Gretna, one of his daughter's wildest fantasies had come to life. She was eloping with a handsome duke.

The Tribbles missed baby George desperately. Why had they not paid him more attention of late? they mourned to each other. Mr Haddon and Mr Randolph missed the baby too. While they played whist of an evening with the sisters, Yvette used to bring the baby down to the drawing room.

Something in the house seemed to have died. Still, they did their bit for Yvette. Both went on calls and loudly mourned the loss of their dressmaker, praised Yvette's skill to the skies and passed around notes with the address of her new shop. They called on Yvette, too, but she was too busy supervising the workmen who were laying out her showroom, and baby George was too fascinated with the jolly company of a plump young nursemaid to make either sister feel wanted.

The news of the elopement rocked London, and although Mr Haddon and Mr Randolph diligently talked about the Tribbles' skill in arranging it, no one believed them. No one believed the duke's mother either. She was surely just trying to smooth things over and make less of a scandal by saying they had all been party to the plot. Lady Bentley had arranged a prestigious marriage for that little nobody, Frederica Sunningdale. She was to marry Lord Alistair Beaumont at a splendid wedding in St James's Chapel. Now *that* was the way things ought to be done, said the wagging tongues.

And so even Effy, who had been so glad to think of relaxing for a whole year without any cares, began to thirst for another success. Amy tried to console her by saying that the duke and his new duchess would return to London and have their great wedding, and faith in them would be restored. But then a letter arrived from Maria in which she said they were boarding a ship at Glasgow to go to France for a honeymoon and not a word of that wedding.

'And that's gratitude for you!' cried Amy, throwing the letter across the room. 'People are so jealous of us; they long to see us fail just because we've snatched so many prizes away from them. By George, I would give anything for just one more success.'

'Alas, Amy,' said Effy sadly. 'I fear our career is at an end. We will bide our time and think of a new line of business.'

'That advertisement has been running for some time now,' said Amy. 'Mr Haddon insisted on paying the costs.'

'The dear man,' cooed Effy, batting her lamp-blackened eyelashes. 'So protective.'

And then she ducked as Amy threw a cushion at her.

Unknown as yet to the Tribbles, their next 'job' was struggling against a gale along the North Cliff of Scarborough in Yorkshire past the cemetery where her parents were buried. The earth on the grave was new, her father having recently gone to join her mother.

Miss Harriet Brown was on her way to visit her aunt, Lady Owen, who lived on the more fashionable St Nicholas Cliff. Harriet had never seen her aunt, although they both lived in the same town. Lady Owen had cut herself off when frivolous Lydia, the belle of Scarborough and Lady Owen's sister, had married a Methodist minister, Mr Thomas Brown, of no particular background what-soever.

So incensed had Lady Owen been at her

sister's fall from grace that she had not even attended her funeral when Lydia died giving birth to baby Harriet.

Harriet had grown up, trained to help her father in his good works and act as unpaid housekeeper. She was now twenty-five and had never been to a ball or party. She did not want to visit her aunt, but Harriet was ever practical and knew her father had left very little money, and that if she did not find help soon, she would end up in the work-house.

The size and splendour of her aunt's mansion rather daunted her, but she reminded herself sternly that this was all mere worldly show and knocked at the great door, feeling the wind plucking at her black mourning-clothes.

When the door opened, she had no card to hand the butler, but merely gave her name.

'You are expected, miss,' said the butler. 'Be so good as to come this way.'

He led the way up a curved staircase and threw open the double doors of a drawing room on the first landing.

'Miss Harriet Brown,' he announced, and then withdrew, leaving Harriet and her aunt together. Each surveyed the other curiously.

Lady Owen saw a tall slim girl dressed in

a shabby black coat and gown and depressing bonnet. She had good eyes, large and sparkling and very blue.

'Take off your bonnet,' she commanded.

Harriet untied the strings and took it off and let it dangle in her hand.

Her hair was magnificent, black and glossy and rippling with natural waves.

Lady Owen noticed, however, that Harriet's chin had a firm, stubborn look and that her mouth was too generous for beauty.

For her part, Harriet saw a woman of fifty or so, very expensively gowned and turbaned with a sour, petulant face. Her eyes were a faded blue and she had very large hairy eyebrows. She smiled and extended her hand. Harriet noticed as Lady Owen smiled that her set of false teeth was of the best china.

'Sit down, Harriet,' said Lady Owen. She waited until Harriet was seated, and then went on. 'I have made inquiries as to your circumstances and find that you have no money, no beaux and no future. Am I right?'

'Yes, Lady Owen.'

'Apart from myself, you are the only surviving member of the Owen family. It is important to me that you should marry well and bear children. Your unfortunate background is known in Scarborough…'

The blue eyes opposite her flashed fire. 'I do not consider my life to date unfortunate,' said Harriet. 'My father was a good and kind man.'

Lady Owen sniffed. 'Don't take on so. I am entitled to my opinion. You are a trifle old but not ill-looking, and it will take a great deal of money and work to make you a suitable bride for some man of high rank. To that end, I am writing to a couple of professional chaperones who reside in London. You will go to them for the Little Season and they will bring you out. You must do your best and learn to charm and flirt.'

Harriet bit back the angry retort that had risen to her lips. She had been brought up to respect her elders. She was shocked at the proposal, but did not know what else to do. She was well educated and had tried to get a position as governess during her father's last illness, but she knew very well she would soon be alone in the world. But several interviews had shown her that the kind of education required was the kind she lacked – Italian, water-colours and piano playing.

'The ladies who will bring you out,' said Lady Owen, 'are called Effy and Amy

Tribble, a couple of farouche eccentrics, who are, nonetheless, of the highest rank of society and are famed for having a gift of refining the seemingly unrefinable.'

While she talked, Harriet sat and assessed her new situation. It was necessary to be practical. It was no use shrinking from the prospect. Her father had taught her there was good in everyone, even Lady Owen. All of London society could not be given over to dissipation and folly. She would find one good man of sober tastes and modest mien, perhaps a member of the clergy, and make the best of it. Her father had always wanted her to marry.

The new Duchess of Berham lay naked in her husband's arms as the ship that was bearing them to France ploughed through the stormy seas.

'Of what are you thinking, my love?' he asked.

'I was thinking of Effy and Amy Tribble,' said Maria. 'They did so want a grand wedding in London and I feel guilty about going on our honeymoon first.'

'The Tribbles will survive.'

Maria stretched and yawned. 'It is a pity Mr Haddon would not marry Miss Amy.

Then they would not have to work.'

'What do you want me to do, my love? Write and order him to do so?'

'Silly. But when we return, perhaps we might call on them and see if we can do anything in that direction.

'As you will. Although the thought of going near Amy Tribble again rather frightens me. You must remember it was she who challenged me to a duel and hit me on the head.'

'And brought us both to our senses,' said Maria.

The ship plunged and shuddered in the trough of a wave and she clutched him hard. 'We will do our best for the Tribble sisters,' he said as his hands slid down her body, 'and we will get to work on that new village. But first... First ... I want you to myself for some little time so that I can do this ... and this ... and this...'

And Maria plunged back into a sea of passion, as noisy and turbulent as the storm outside.

Miss Spiggs was walking through the lanes outside Bath, feeling very sorry for herself. The Kendalls had dispensed with her services. She thirsted for revenge on the Tribbles, for she was sure it was they who had poisoned dear Mrs Kendall's mind against her.

The sound of a noisy, haranguing voice reached her ears, and she came out of her bitter thoughts to see she was approaching some sort of meeting that was being held in a field. A man was standing on a platform, speaking to a small crowd.

Miss Spiggs stopped to listen. 'Brothers and sisters,' said the speaker, 'why should there be one law for the rich and one for the poor? Why should we have to slave all our days for people who are no better than we?'

He was wearing a very tight blue coat with brass buttons over a striped waistcoat. A beaver hat was perched on his ginger hair. Miss Spiggs thought him a compelling figure and edged her way to the front of the crowd until she was standing below him. 'They ride past us in their carriages and never notice the poor starving in the streets,' said the speaker, as he dropped a quick calculating glance at Miss Spiggs, discreet in dove-grey silk gown with the diamond pin Maria had given her winking on the front of it.

'And it is not only the very poor who suffer,' he said and now his eyes seemed to hold those of Miss Spiggs. 'It is the poor relations, the cast-off companions, the wretches who

231

have only their dignity to live on. Let us pray for them too, brothers and sisters.'

How true, thought Miss Spiggs, engulfed in a pleasurable wave of self-pity.

At the end of his speech, the orator said a collection would be taken up for The Brothers and Sisters of the Uprising of the Underdog. He swept off his hat and passed it round. Miss Spiggs ostentatiously put in a bright new shilling and hoped he noticed.

The meeting ended with the singing of a hymn, and the crowd began to shuffle away. Miss Spiggs was just turning away when she found the speaker at her elbow.

'Allow me to introduce myself, my lady,' he said with a low bow. 'I am Dr Frank.'

Miss Spiggs tittered. 'I am not titled, sir, but one of those poor companions you mentioned in your speech.'

'Indeed!' His eyes shone with warm sympathy. 'You must tell me about it. There is an inn hard by and I would be honoured if you would join me in some refreshment.'

His wife approached him bearing the hat. 'Excuse me,' he said to Miss Spiggs, 'while I talk to my assistant.'

He snatched the hat from his wife, Bessie, tipped the coins out and put them in his pocket.

'Lose yourself, Bess,' he hissed. 'See that diamond pin? I'll have it off her by the end of the day. So you ain't my wife.'

Bessie nodded, although she sent a venomous look in Miss Spiggs's direction.

By the time Dr Frank and Miss Spiggs had reached the inn, she had told him all about the perfidy of the Tribbles.

And Frank, the Tribbles' ex-footman, put aside for the moment any idea of getting that diamond pin right away. Here was a coincidence. Here was a rare happening. He pretended he had never heard of the Tribbles while he asked question after question. Although his leaving the sisters' household had been of his own doing, he blamed them for all his subsequent bad luck. There must be some way he could use this silly woman to avenge himself on them and get not only that diamond pin from Miss Spiggs but money from the Tribbles as well. He remembered seeing Amy in St Charles Street but was sure she had not recognized him. He had become a fine gentleman, he thought proudly, squinting down at the silk of his showy waistcoat and the gold tassels on his boots, and, in any case, London was a better hunting-ground.

Amy and Effy were seated with Mr Randolph and Mr Haddon some two weeks later, discussing the surprising letter that had arrived from Lady Owen.

'Do you remember her, Effy?' asked Amy. 'She had a beautiful sister – Lydia, that was it. Young Lord Lamperton was enamoured of her, as were quite a few gentlemen, but she showed no interest and they left their one Season, both of them unwed. It seems, gentlemen, that Lydia married a Methodist preacher and it is their daughter Lady Owen wants to send us. There seems to be no fault in the girl, except that she is a leetle old – twenty-five – and unpolished. "Modest and well-behaved if a trifle stiff in her manner and disgracefully short of light conversation," says Lady Owen. Seems easy enough.'

Effy shifted restlessly. 'It would have been so nice to forget about these wretched girls for a little,' she said with a sigh, 'but if we could secure a good marriage for a Methodist – Methodist, mark you – minister's daughter, then we should prove our worth. What do you think, Mr Randolph?'

Mr Randolph looked pleased. He was used to both sisters consulting Mr Haddon first. 'It seems quite safe,' he said. 'I think you should go ahead with it.'

Although the sisters agreed with him, he

could sense a sudden coldness in the room and wondered what he had said wrong.

When the gentlemen had left, Amy said, 'They both sit there, two rich nabobs, drinking our hard-earned wine, eating our hard-earned cakes and agreeing placidly on more work for us. Oh, why does not just one of them say, "Be mine"?'

Effy stretched out her hand and Amy clutched it. Outside the hoarse voice of the watch called the hour and strains of a waltz filtered through from the house next door where the neighbours were holding a ball.

They sat like that for a long time, each one thinking of the long years of parties and balls and routs, the endless parade of gentlemen who just might be interested, the hopes and fears and disappointments – so very many disappointments.

Amy cleared her throat and tried to think of something to say to lighten the gloom. 'You know, Effy, when I was in St Charles Street, there was some fellow rousing the crowd to riot. I saw a handbill which said he was Dr Frank and then I saw him, up a lamp-post, staring at me. And do you know who it was? Our Frank. That silly footman who tried to get the rest of the servants to stop work.'

Effy sat silently, her throat working. A tear rolled down her cheek.

'Hey, what is this, sister? A wake? Champagne, Harris!' shouted Amy. 'We drink a toast to our future, Effy. We're still alive, which is more than you can say for most of our contemporaries, and damme, if we ain't got two real live gentlemen callers.'

'We have?'

'Course we do. Aren't Mr Haddon and Mr Randolph here practically every day? We've got the pleasures of company without the pain of marriage. Why, that old trout, Lady Witherspoon, said t'other day, "I think Effy Tribble must go in for witchcraft. She gets younger by the minute." And did you mark last time we drove in the Park that Colonel Flanders actually *leered* at you?'

'He did?' Effy released Amy's hand and patted her silvery hair.

'You're an awful old rip, Effy,' said Amy Tribble.

Effy giggled. 'And I will tell you something, sister. I think Mr Haddon's in love with you. There!'

A sort of radiance illuminated Amy's plain face. 'Hey, here's the champagne. Call the staff in, Harris. Give them all a glass. A celebration.'

'May I ask the nature of the celebration?' asked Harris.

'Life!' said Amy Tribble. 'There's life in the old dogs yet. Or should I say bitches?'

'Oh, *Amy*,' admonished her exasperated sister.

This Large Print Book, for people
who cannot read normal print,
is published under the auspices of

THE ULVERSCROFT FOUNDATION